WEDDING NIGHTMARE

A MYSTERY-PSYCHOLOGICAL THRILLER

SUSAN SPECHT ORAM

SOS COMMUNICATIONS

WEDDING NIGHTMARE

A Mystery-Psychological Thriller

Susan Specht Oram

SOS Communications LLC

This book is a work of fiction. Names, characters, businesses, organizations, events, and places other than those clearly in the public domain, are either a product of the author's imagination or are used fictitiously. Any semblance to actual persons, living or dead, events or locales is entirely coincidental.

WEDDING NIGHTMARE Copyright © 2026 by Susan Specht Oram. All rights reserved. No part of this publication may be reproduced, stored in any retrieval system, or transmitted, in any form by any means, electronic, mechanical, photocopying, recording or otherwise, without prior written permission from the publisher except in the case of brief quotations embodied in critical articles and reviews.

Published by SOS Communications LLC in 2026

NO AI TRAINING: Without in any way limiting the author's and publisher's exclusive rights under copyright, any use of this publication to "train" generative artificial intelligence (AI) technologies to generate text is expressly prohibited. The author reserves all rights to license uses of this work for generative AI training and development of machine learning language models.

www.susanspechtoram.com

First Edition

ISBN ebook: 979-8-9937061-4-6

ISBN paperback: 979-8-9937061-5-3

 Formatted with Vellum

1

BELLE

Hurrying between office buildings, a steady breeze brushed past my cheeks. My friend Kitty stopped to chat, and I tapped a toe. I had a meeting to run and didn't want to be late. Behind her, Gas Works Park loomed at the north end of Lake Union in Seattle.

She smiled. "Have you heard? Ralph and Claire are getting married."

I tightened my grip on my leather briefcase. Ralph broke up with me at a restaurant, ignoring the fact we'd already set our wedding date, and I've been seething about it ever since. I suspect he was already two-timing me, as he started seeing Claire twelve hours later.

My friend touched my arm. "I'm sorry if I upset you. I thought you were over him, or I wouldn't have brought it up."

I forced a smile, suppressing my building rage. "Oh, I'm fine. I was just thinking about my mom. She's having a hard time these days. But I wish Ralph and Claire the best."

We said goodbye, and I hurried away, envisioning ways I might possibly ruin their event. It'd be my pleasure to wreck Ralph's carefully crafted life and make their wedding a nightmare.

2

MEG

The bride, a woman in her early thirties from the city, stomped her foot on the farmhouse wood floor, where I catered weddings. Her face was flushed, her freckles stood out, which was not a good look on her wedding day, and she clenched a fist. "I want a spotlight aimed at us when we take our vows."

I said, "I'm sorry, but I'm in charge of catering. I'll get someone in events management to talk to you about lighting."

She glowered, face red with fury. My eyes flitted around the room, looking for help. I hoped she wouldn't keel over and faint, or have a heart attack.

Motioning with my hands to calm her down, I said, "We want your special day to be perfect. I'll have someone take care of this right away."

I took a deep breath to calm myself and counted down

the hours until the wedding party would end. We'd say goodbye, lock the doors, clean up and run home to collapse, returning to do it all over again another day.

I strode away before she could unleash more angst and panic over the upcoming event. Like many off-island brides holding a wedding at The Farm, she was eager to wrestle details into perfection, even if they were already just right. Being queen for a day meant exerting control over everything and everyone in sight, and I preferred to stay in the background as much as possible.

I rolled my eyes, aware of the irony that although I owned a catering company serving weddings, I'm divorced. Biff and I had a picture-perfect ceremony, right here in this place. But our marriage ended in disaster when he walked out one Christmas Eve, leaving two stunned young kids and me, a weeping wife, behind.

I shook my head at how he left beautiful Barnacle Island. Biff's aloof mother told me when I called looking for him that he'd driven to his hometown of Mill Valley, California and moved into an apartment building she owned. He never worked, which was a source of contention between us before he disappeared.

I waved a hand in front of my face. Good riddance to him. Any man who doesn't stick around for his two beautiful children and stay in touch is a royal jerk.

Knocking on the event managers office door, I relayed the bride's request.

Candy nodded at her desk. "I'll get right on it. Thanks

for telling me. I think this event is going to be a challenge, but I hope I'm wrong."

Before going in the kitchen, I stopped at an open door and gazed out at wild meadows and pastures surrounding the property. Inhaling the sweet aroma of fresh hay, I hoped to absorb some of the tranquility and add it to the essence of my food.

The bride cried out, "I smell manure. Someone do something!"

I hustled into the kitchen and released a sigh. Thankfully, in my domain, I could hide from what appeared to be a brewing bridal storm. The events manager, Candy, rushed past, heading toward the frantic bride.

I glanced at a white wall clock and nodded. We had seven hours to go until this shindig ended. I bit my lower lip and hoped nothing would go wrong with my part of the event.

My daughter rushed into the room, her curly dark brown hair bouncing with each step. "I made it just in time."

I went over and gave her a quick hug. Stepping back, I smiled. She and her brother were the best part of my marriage. With every ounce of my being, I tried to make up for the missing parent and heal the trauma of their past, but I knew I'd never be enough. He up and left one Christmas Eve, without saying goodbye, or telling us he was moving from our island in the rainy but beautiful Pacific Northwest. Like many from California, he complained about the winter gray weather and I guess he couldn't cope.

Patting Francesca's shoulder, I said, "You're ten minutes late, but I'll overlook it this time. Now tie back your hair, put on an apron and let's get going."

"Sure thing, Mom."

Francesca pulled up her hair in a ponytail and slipped a green apron over her head. I pursed my lips, recalling how at times, she was uncoordinated. I hoped she wouldn't trip while serving dinner.

3

FRANCESCA

I ran from my car and breezed into the kitchen at The Farm, breathing hard. I grinned at my mom, who hired me to help cater weddings, and opened my arms. "I'm here. Right on time."

Mom frowned, crossing her arms. "Actually, you're ten minutes late. Try to be on time for tomorrow's wedding."

"I had to park in the back lot, so it took longer than I expected."

Mom's brow furrowed. "It's your first day, and watch out for the bride, because she's freaking out. Whatever you do, don't get on her bad side."

I shrugged. "Sure, how hard can it be to serve people at a wedding?"

Mom said, "Just remember what we reviewed last night in our practice session."

I rolled my eyes. "I did fine on the practice runs and didn't trip once. It'll be fine. Don't worry."

Mom looked away but not before I saw a flicker of concern cross her face. My brother, who was also working the event and filling in because someone called in sick, was the easy-going one. It was easier for me to get my feelings hurt, with my face reflecting how I felt.

Mom said, "Start with the place settings and do it like I showed you."

"Sure, Mom, and thanks for the work. I could really use the money."

I smiled and went out to the dining room, folding cloth napkins. I hoped this job would help me adopt a new attitude. I'd been stuck in the past for far too long, and I needed a new outlook on life.

Movement outside the windows facing a grassy area, with pastures and a meadow beyond that, caught my attention. A woman in her early thirties in jeans and a shirt jabbed an index finger at gray clouds on the horizon. I winced and got back to work.

4

MEG

A van pulled up outside, and a woman hopped out, ambling into my workspace with her hands in her denim overall pockets. A tiny diamond in her nostril sparkled, reflecting light. She pulled her hair back in a ponytail and brushed a strand of brown hair from her face. "I'm here to deliver the cake. Sorry I'm late. Traffic on I-5 was worse than I expected. Where do you want it?"

I said, "I'll check with the events manager. She'll want to see you."

I radioed Candy, but she didn't respond. My son Troy chopped vegetables with a vengeance, with his back to us. I'd hired him to help for the day, because my employee called in sick at the last minute. Pressure was building, and it wasn't only coming from the worried bride. Something felt off today. Little things going wrong were adding up.

Over coffee this morning, I'd read the weather forecast. A storm was coming, bringing wind and rain. I doubted any bride would be happy about that, not one bit.

I radioed Candy a second time. She picked up and when I said the cake was here, she said, "Can you handle it? I'm outside with the bride and can't step away. You know where the cake goes, on the table in the corner."

I said, "Sure thing."

The delivery person looked around the commercial kitchen, eyes lingering on my son's sandy short hair and his biceps. He worked as a baker, although he had a law degree, and in the early hours before dawn, he worked out lifting weights at home.

With a shrug, I said, "I'll show you where to put the cake. Do you need help getting it out of the van?"

"Definitely. This cake is a monster and very delicate. I can't move it on my own."

"Troy can help you."

I went over and patted my son on the shoulder. He looked up with a smile, pulling out his earbuds. I was lucky my two grown kids decided to live on Barnacle Island, where they had grown up.

I said, "The cake's here. Will you help her bring it in?"

He nodded to the delivery gal, who was about his age, in her early thirties. "Show us where to put it. We'll bring it in."

"Follow me." I strode out to the main event area. Dark wood beams in the ceiling gave the remodeled farmhouse a rustic feeling. A wood floor added an element of warmth. The sky was becoming overcast, perhaps a harbinger of weather to come, and clouds covered the sun.

The bride's shrill voice carried from outside. "I can't have clouds on my wedding day. I picked a day when I was guaranteed sunshine. This isn't right."

I arched my eyebrows but kept quiet about the brewing bridal storm. By the time the ceremony started, the bride may have forgotten her worries about creating the perfect event. We try our best at The Farm, but life happens and most events contain one or two tiny errors, like a bride sneezing because of certain flowers in her wedding bouquet, or guests rushing inside during a sudden downpour. It's our job to put the polish on those surprise elements of potential disaster and turn chaos into a perfect shining moment.

I frowned as a concern crossed my mind. My daughter, Francesca, was known to be slightly clumsy at times. I'd hired her to sail elegantly through dinner service. Surely she could carry plates to tables without a problem. I'd even gone so far as to practice at home with her last night, and she passed the test. I told her last night, "The power of positive thinking helps. Picture yourself doing it perfectly, and it'll be a breeze."

She smiled. "Don't worry. Waiting tables will be easy, and I'll be the best wait person you've ever had."

Now, I pointed to a table covered with a white cloth in a corner. "That's the designated place for the cake. But the bride's nerves are already frayed, so be careful. We don't want one iota of a problem with the cake."

Troy said, "No problem, Mom. Don't worry. This'll be fine."

The young woman said, "I helped bake it, and it's beautiful."

They went out to the van, and I nodded to myself. All would be right with the world today, no matter what the weather. My two grown kids were working with me, and we got along, despite their dad ditching us years ago.

I watched as Troy and the bakery delivery gal brought in a large sheet cake decorated with a forest setting. A brown stump and green trees graced the edges. On top of that, they added three round cakes, each with smaller dimensions than the one below. Reaching up, she added a tall, tilting cake on top. Grinning, she stepped back.

I crossed my arms. "Well done. It looks like a birch tree in a forest."

Troy said, "It's amazing. Look how the white bark is peeling off the tree. It's beautiful."

The baker beamed. "That's what the bride wanted. She asked for a tall birch tree in a forest, with peeling bark. I think we nailed it, but it was a challenge."

Troy said, "It must've been tricky to make it so tall,

with part of the tree leaning over at the top. I would've thought it'd slide off or break apart, but it looks fine to me."

The baker grinned. "Thanks. It was a challenge, and I'm pleased with how it turned out."

I said goodbye and turned away, but Troy lingered to chat with the baker. Going back in the kitchen, I smiled. Their shared love of baking might be a bond bringing them together.

In the kitchen, I studied the menu. The bride insisted on serving a creamy butternut squash soup and a mixed salad with dried cranberries and fresh farm-grown greens for the first course. She asked for sourdough dinner rolls, which Troy made and brought with him. The bride wanted to replicate her first meal with the groom at a Seattle restaurant near the waterfront.

Hauling out a huge stewpot, I added chicken stock, heavy cream, curry spices and butter, stirring the soup. Sprinkling in ginger, sage and rosemary, I inhaled the aroma of happiness in a bowl. Weddings reminded me of how my kids and I haven't been very successful in love. Their dad's disappearance left us with our own challenges with trust. I hope this bride has better luck with love than I did.

Out of the corner of my eye, I noticed Francesca looking at something but I focused on my tasks. She didn't need my supervision to set tables, and I had loads of work to do.

5

TROY

I exchanged phone numbers with the baker who created a fantastic once-in-a-lifetime wedding cake, and we said goodbye. But I knew I'd probably never contact her. The island seemed like a separate world from the mainland, and I had everything I needed on Barnacle Island, where I grew up. I wouldn't take the ferry or drive over the Deception Pass Bridge to hang out with anyone.

In the kitchen, Mom and I seamlessly glided past and stepped around each other, avoiding a collision. We've danced this cooking waltz since I was young, and I helped her make meals. Back then, I was curious and wanted to learn to cook to better understand how ingredients combined to make certain flavors. But I also wanted to lift part of her burden as a single mom. She was tired most of the time when we were growing up.

I stopped shredding lettuce and studied Mom's face.

Her cheeks were rosy, and she glowed with health. She worked hard and at home, she loved to garden, even in the rain. Nothing stops my mom.

My older sister, Francesca, appeared. "I have to tell you something."

Mom bumped into Franny's hip and said, "I didn't see you there. Next time, announce yourself when you come in and don't stand where we're working."

Franny moved toward the door. "Sorry, I didn't know."

I pressed my lips together and hoped this wouldn't be my sister's last day working for Mom. That's the last thing she'd need. When Dad left us, he stole Franny's easy laughter and light-hearted attitude, and I took on the job of protecting my sister's feelings. Dad told us when he dies, my sister and I will each inherit an apartment building, and we'll be set for life. That's why I felt fine enrolling in law school and taking on student debt, because I knew I'd pay it off one day. But Franny took the news about our coming into money as meaning she could coast through life, working part-time and living on little until she struck it rich.

Mom said, "How do the dining tables look? Is everything set?"

Franny frowned. "I set the tables and the bride came in and loved it. But something's wrong with the cake."

Mom said in an impatient voice, "What do you mean?"

Franny pointed to the dining room. "I think I saw the cake sliding, just barely. The tilted top of the tree might be slightly moving and about to fall down. You know, the tilted part of the cake?"

Mom's eyes opened wide.

My mouth dropped open. The cake baker was long gone and might be on the mainland by now. We couldn't let the wedding cake splat to the floor. No one would forget it, and Mom's catering business would fold. I had to protect Mom's business and the bride's special day.

I hurried to the dining room to prevent disaster.

A scream rang out.

6

CLAIRE, THE BRIDE

Gray clouds gathered, and I flung my hands in the air, wailing at invisible weather gods. I picked this date because, according to forecasts, this would be a sunny summer day. I started planning my wedding when I was five and practiced walking down the aisle with my best friend Brandy. We argued about who'd be the bride, and my mother stomped down the basement stairs and burst into my musty bedroom, pointing a finger and telling us to take turns, or she'd send Brandy home. I sighed, pulled off my pink tutu and handed it over for her to wear.

I squinted at a dark storm cloud scudding overhead, and a feeling of dread swept over me, giving me the chills. Goosebumps pricked my skin, a breeze kicked up, and I rubbed my arms. One day, when we were on an extended trip in our camper van, Mom packed her things and left.

Dad told me we were continuing our adventure, just the two of us. It was fun for a few years, but when I turned seventeen, I told him our journey was over. I called my maternal grandmother in Seattle and asked if I could live with her. She said yes, and I began a new life in the big city, leaving my nomadic childhood behind.

Putting my hands on my bony hips, I frowned. My cousin Lacey sent two greeting cards in lavender-scented envelopes. Four months ago, I received her first missive. She sent a greeting card with a drawing of a tiger on the front and, on the inside, she wrote in flowery cursive writing that she was angry she wasn't picked to be in the wedding party. She wrote, 'I hope you'll include me in the wedding party, and if possible, make me maid of honor. You have two weeks to correct your mistake.'

Meadow grass swayed in a stiffening breeze. A canopy flapped in the wind. I hadn't changed my mind. My friend Rhonda, who was going to be maid of honor, was the best person for the job, and I remained steadfast in my choice of bridesmaids. It was Team Rhonda, all the way. Rhonda was a whirlwind of fun and a pro at organizing events. But she wasn't here when I needed her. Rhonda was stuck on the mainland, waiting for a ferry. She'd texted her apologies, saying the first ferry was cancelled due to staffing shortages and the next boat had a mechanical issue that needed to be fixed.

I swallowed hard, recalling Cousin Lacey's second card. We met once when Dad and I passed through Burns,

Oregon, and she waitressed at a diner where we ate. She carried a chip on her shoulder from the moment I met her, and she said she was jealous I was traveling with my dad. But at fifteen, I thought she was lucky to be planted in one place, not having to move around and search for free spots to park our van each night.

In Lacey's second letter, stuck inside a Mother's Day card, she wrote if I didn't ditch my maid of honor and pick her, or at least put her in the wedding party, I'd learn there were consequences for being rude. I ripped up the card and tossed it in the trash, not wanting a bad omen lingering, overshadowing my hopes for my upcoming wedding.

I chewed on my lip, because her words worried me. What if she showed up at my wedding and ruined it? But no one would be that cold-hearted and deranged.

Shaking my head, I sauntered into the dining room to be sure all was ready. Even though The Farm had an event planner, I wanted to be on site and make sure everything was just right. Rolling over miles of paved roads in the van with Dad, I dreamed of this day. I'd wanted to live in one place with someone who loved me, and I found that in my best friend of a fiancé. I'd told Ralph to stay away from The Farm today until I texted him to say all was well, and I was getting ready in the bridal suite.

Gliding into the dining hall, I nodded at the pristine white cloths covering long tables and bunches of fresh-cut lavender in pewter vases.

"Great job," I said to a catering person, whose dark

curly hair was up in a ponytail. If she hadn't pulled back her hair, I would've told her to wear a hair net, because no way would I allow a stray strand of hair to appear in my guest's food. Nothing gross and disgusting would happen today, because I'd made sure it would run smoothly.

Turning to my marvelous wedding cake, I grinned. But a slight movement caught my attention. My mouth dropped open, and to my horror, the bent top portion of the birch tree started to droop.

I tilted my head and stared, because maybe I was imagining seeing a slight movement. I hadn't eaten today in order to fit into my backless white lace low cut wedding dress. It was one size too small, but it'd look fabulous in wedding photos in the years to come.

I gulped. The top part of the cake resembling a tree branch was definitely moving. My beautiful wedding cake was about to slide down and go splat on the floor.

My heart raced, and my hands went cold. I screamed at the top of my lungs. "Someone help, come quick! The cake is falling."

7

FRANCESCA

I ran toward the dining room, following my brother. It crossed my mind that maybe I wasn't well suited to catering. Unlike my brother Troy, I wasn't intensely on task or engaging with strangers. I'm more of the take-it-easy kind of person who wanders through life. But I need this job to pay my rent, so I'll stick it out. I'd rather be sipping margaritas and living in an old house I've had my eye on. The place is packed with a hoarder's stash of trash, and it's been sitting on the market for a long time. If the place is still for sale when Dad dies, I'll try to buy the hoarder's house, clear it out and enjoy life by the water, kicking up my feet and watching sunsets.

I entered the dining room and clapped a hand over my mouth. The top of the tall cake resembling a leaning tree was starting to slowly slide. Gravity was doing its job, pulling down the top hanging branch with peeling frosting bark toward the floor.

The bride pointed with a trembling finger, "The cake is sliding. Please, stop it, before it's too late."

Troy rushed over and gently lifted the front of the cake about two inches, and the tilting tree became still.

Troy said, "Find something to stick as a wedge under the front of the cake."

Mom looked around, flustered.

Wanting to be helpful, I said, "I'll find something."

I hurried in the kitchen, grabbed a wooden cutting board and took it to Troy. I said, "Mom, okay if we use this?"

She nodded. "Fine. Do it now, before the top of the cake falls off."

The bride bit her lip, wringing her hands. "Please, fix it. Do something."

Troy said, "Franny, tuck it under while I hold it up."

I slipped the board under the front of the cake, and he let go. We stepped back, and everyone in the room issued a collective sigh.

Mom said to the bride, "The cake should be fine now. But don't let anyone dance or stomp on the floor near the cake until the top layer is removed, and it's cut."

The bride said, "I was very particular about how the cake should look, and I insisted the baker follow my drawing exactly. But we almost ended up with a mess because of my design. What a disaster that would've been."

With a nod, I considered how we sometimes squeeze life's moments hard, seeking control, but crush a serendipitous moment or creation by somebody else. I patted my brother on the back. "Good job. You saved the day, like you always do."

He blushed and scratched his stubbled chin. "Anyone would've done what I did."

Mom chimed in. "Great work. We got here just in time. Too bad the baker wasn't here to see what happened."

The bride's phone rang, and she walked outside.

Mom said in a low voice, "I guess the customer isn't always right, not when designing a one-off wedding cake."

A middle-aged woman wearing an events manager name tag with the name Candy and a navy-blue pantsuit strode in. She ran a hand through her short blond hair and said in a low voice, "I thought I'd seen it all before, but this bride takes the cake."

Mom nodded. "We almost had a wedding cake disaster, but it's fixed. Make sure the guests know not to stomp on the floor or dance near the cake until we serve it. The top part looks ready to topple and fall on the floor."

The events manager cringed. "We can't let anything go wrong. The bride's nerves are frayed as it is. Her bridal party is stuck waiting for a ferry in Mukilteo, and she's freaking out about the change in the weather."

I opened my hands. "As anyone would be in her situation. Do you have a back-up plan for if it rains?"

Candy tilted her head. "We do. And you are?"

Mom smiled, gesturing to me. "This is my daughter Francesca. She's helping me out today and starting a career in catering."

The events manager smiled. "Welcome to my world of stress. Nice to meet you. I'm Candy. Now I've got to make sure the tents for cocktail hour are adequately anchored, in case the wind picks up. We don't want them blowing away."

Candy hurried outside, and Mom turned to me, frowning. "You shouldn't speak to guests or members of the staff unless they address you first. We're hierarchical at The Farm, despite appearances of laid-back charm. Understood?"

I winced. Mom was kind, but at work she became bossy. I thought this would be an easy gig, but instead I'd stepped into what felt like controlled chaos. Catering events probably wasn't my calling, and I'd look for another job soon. Tomorrow, I'd stop at the garden store in Bayview to see if they were hiring.

I swallowed my pride, wanting to keep this job until something better came along. "You bet. I've got it, Mom."

My brother gave me a wink, lifting my spirits, and we followed Mom into the kitchen. I whispered to Troy, "I don't think I'm cut out for this kind of work. Too much drama and stress."

Troy squeezed my hand. "Just keep going, Franny. One step at a time. We'll get through this wedding, and the one tomorrow, and the day after that. You'll get the hang of it."

I pursed my lips. "I hope so, but I kind of doubt it."

He scratched his chin. "You've run through a lot of jobs since high school. There aren't many places left for you to work on the island. Stick it out and change your frame of mind. Working for Mom won't be that bad."

I glanced over at her and said to Troy in a low voice, "She's a dragon in the kitchen with her claws out about everything. I miss being around normal Mom."

Mom said, "I'm your boss Mom, the catering monster. That's enough chit-chat between you two. Let's get to work. We have a wedding to cater."

8

CLAIRE, THE BRIDE

I stepped outside and texted my father. 'Are u on the ferry? Did you pick up Grandma?'

He replied, 'She's with me, but the ferry is delayed. First it was staffing issues. Now mechanical problems.'

I sucked in a breath. I needed them here beside me. They'd be a calming force in the face of the cake drama and the change in weather. I wanted them as a buffer to fend off Cousin Lacey, if she showed up. I gritted my teeth. I never should have invited Lacey in the first place. That's when the trouble started. Did she put a curse on the wedding, with her negative attitude? My hands trembled with worry about her vague threats.

I texted Dad, 'Have you heard from Lacey? I hope she won't show up.'

'Nope. Not a word.'

I chewed on my lower lip. 'Can you drive around and over Deception Pass Bridge and skip the ferry? We only have three hours until the wedding.'

'Too late for that. We'll stick with the original plan. They'll get it fixed in time.'

'I hope so.'

'Love you pumpkin. Stay calm. We'll be there as soon as we can.'

My throat closed tight with tears. I shouldn't have picked a venue on an island for my wedding. I shouldn't have assumed it wouldn't rain. I should have told Dad and my bridesmaids to drive north and take the big beautiful old bridge instead of relying on the State ferry system.

I swallowed tears and typed, 'Love you too.'

Slipping the phone into my pocket, I sighed. At least my soon-to-be-husband was on Barnacle Island. Of that, I was sure. I wouldn't text or call Ralph about my troubles. I'd turn this impending fiasco into a day mirroring my long-held dreams, even if I had to strangle every iota of the event into submission.

Rain drizzled down, getting my hair wet. I groaned and put my hands over my head, running toward the farmhouse. I thought friends and family would swarm around the place early, but I was alone without a single friendly soul in sight.

9

CANDY, EVENTS MANAGER

The bride stood in the dining room studying the cake. I said, "Don't worry. We'll watch it like a hawk. Nothing will happen to it."

I hurried into my office and sat at my desk, calling the baker responsible for the cake near-disaster. The baker needed to know not to let customers talk them into creating a cake that wasn't tenable. A sliding cake? No, thanks. One featuring a tree branch tipping over? Definitely not.

When the baker answered the phone, I drummed my fingers on the desk and said, "Yasmin, do you have a moment?"

"Sure. What's up?"

"The cake almost went kaput on the floor."

"Oh, no, what happened?"

Claire, the bride, paced outside my office door, and I lowered my voice. No need to rattle the poor woman. This was her special day, but she was alone. Ferries to the island were down and wouldn't be fixed for two to three hours at earliest. I needed to talk with Claire about how long she'd wait for her guests, and if she wanted to proceed with the ceremony as scheduled.

I stood and a movement outside the window caught my attention. A red-headed woman in her early-thirties skulked around the back of the building, crouching low, hunched over and wearing a black hooded cape. Her thick red hair flowed down to her waist and swayed as she moved..

Clearing my throat, I said to the baker in an urgent, low voice, "The top part that tilts was sliding down. We propped up the front of the cake, so it's okay for now. Maybe next time use a simple, traditional design, so we don't have to worry about it falling on the floor."

Yasmin gasped. "I'm sorry about that. Yes, I'll keep that in mind in the future. Do you want me to come back and fix it?"

The bride knocked on my door and stepped inside my office, waving at me and flashing a tense smile.

I said, "No, I think we've got it under control. Or at least I hope so."

Yasmin said, "Good, because I'm about to drive over Deception Pass Bridge and didn't exactly want to turn around. The ferry system is having problems, so I'm driving to Seattle."

We said goodbye and hung up, and I stood, smiling widely at Claire, the poor abandoned bride. Things weren't going her way today, but I'd do everything I could to bring her joy. She and her fiancé Ralph had spent a bundle on booking The Farm for her wedding, and she deserved to have the best day possible. I'd leap over tall buildings to deliver the experience she wanted.

I said, "I'm glad to see you. I have unfortunate news about the ferry system, and we need to discuss delaying the wedding ceremony, the cocktail hour and dinner and dancing."

Her face went pale, and she gnawed on her lower lip. With a nod, she said, "I heard about the delays, and I'd like everyone here before I walk down the aisle. And it's raining, so we need to move it inside. What's your best guess about when everyone will get here?"

I crossed my arms and sighed. "Sadly, it may take people three hours or more to arrive. We just don't know at this point. The ferry said they're working on it, but two boats are out."

She tilted her head. "So if we move the ceremony back three hours, that puts dinner at what time? Ten at night? That's too late."

I nodded. "The chef would have a fit if we did that, but it's possible. It's up to you. There'll also be overtime charges associated with the catering service, staff and facilities, so you might consider that before you make a decision. And the boats stop running at a certain time at night."

She tapped her lips. "If we serve dinner late, we'd finish up when? One in the morning? I'd hate to see my guests driving at that time of night after drinking for hours. If they're staying in Seattle, could they even catch a ferry at that time of the morning?"

I shook my head. "No, the last boat leaves Clinton at twelve-thirty-five, and the ferries are down until four-forty in the morning. So, that won't work for guests needing to head back to Seattle tonight."

She walked over to the window, peering out. "So we could wait for people to show up, hold a quick ceremony, skip serving dinner, which we already paid for, and then the guests run to catch a ferry back to Mukilteo. I really don't like that idea. It's not what I planned or wanted, and it doesn't allow time to celebrate and hang out together. Or, we could go ahead and not deviate from the plan, but I'd be taking a chance of missing my Dad, and grandmother, and maid of honor, and others we invited."

Tears trickled down her cheeks. She wiped her eyes and said, "I can't make this decision on my own. I need Ralph's input. I didn't want to see him today before the wedding, and he's staying in a cottage in a hollow where there's no cell or internet reception. I guess I'll have to drive over to see him and talk this over. What a disaster this is turning out to be."

I stepped over to her. "I'm sorry things are rotten for you today, of all days. It's not fair. It's not right, and it shouldn't be happening. You deserve a perfect day, with family and friends surrounding you."

She blew out a breath and nodded. "Thanks."

Outside, a redhead wearing a cape ran past, carrying a green canvas satchel crossways over her shoulder and a large slingshot in her right hand. She ran into the meadow and disappeared from sight.

Claire gasped and pointed outside. In a trembling voice, she said, "Did you see her? That's my cousin Lacey, and she's angry I didn't include her in the wedding party."

I cringed, picturing the redhead stirring up trouble at an event I oversaw. I'd be in trouble if the redhead ruined Claire's wedding. Our brand specialized in offering a serene, satisfying experience, and that's why brides recommended The Farm to their friends. I needed to protect our reputation and stop the woman from wrecking the wedding.

My throat was dry, and I cleared my throat. "Would you like me to call the police, and they'll ask her to leave? We don't want her disturbing the peace on your wedding day."

She tapped an index finger to her cheek. "I have an idea. Let me talk to Ralph, but I think there's no need to call the police. I'll come back with our decision about the timing for the ceremony. Thanks for the talk."

She strode out of my office with her jaw set, tapping into her phone.

I stared at the meadow but saw no signs of a would-be trouble maker. I had a feeling this would be a day that would live on in our memories as breaking records of things going wrong and weird.

10

CLAIRE, THE BRIDE

I hurried out of the event manager's office and stopped in the dining room for a moment to check on the cake before going to see Ralph. Rain pattered against the window panes. I stood back and studied the cake to make sure it was stable, the way my husband-to-be and I are meant to be.

I tapped my foot, keeping time with my racing heartbeat. My careful plan was tossed aside because of cancelled ferry boats. The events manager needs to know soon what we want to do.

I whispered to myself, "This is not how I wanted today to go, and it's bad luck. I hope this is the last of our problems."

I hurried out to my car and headed to the rental cottage, windshield wipers swiping back and forth, just like my life is today. I hoped Ralph would be at the cottage. We needed to get this sorted out right away.

11

RALPH, THE GROOM

I leaned over the sink, splashing cold rusty-brown water on my face. With a groan, I mumbled, "I drank too much last night."

I stumbled down a hall in the vacation rental and collapsed in an easy chair in the living room. Scratching my wrist, I said to my best man, Mack, "We shouldn't have tied one on so late last night. I'm still drunk."

He grinned, showing his crooked front teeth. "Make a note for the next time. We're wiped out, but it was worth it."

My head throbbed, and I didn't bother to answer.

He said, "I had a great time pounding back beers with the locals. One was an actual logger. Can you believe it? The other guy plants trees for a living."

I closed my eyes. "Maybe holding my bachelor party the night before my wedding wasn't the best idea."

"But it's the only way it worked for our schedules. I had to fly in from Thailand."

Massaging my temples, I moaned. "You could've flown in a few days earlier."

He yawned. "I had a podcast series scheduled and couldn't move the dates."

I frowned, feeling surly. I'd been the one to pay for our party last night. Acid churned in my gut. "I gave you eleven month's notice."

He snored, and I drifted off into dreams.

Mack snorted, waking me up. I stretched my arms and smiled, looking around the cottage I rented on a dirt lane. Today was going to be the best day of my life, because I was getting married.

But then I remembered my former girlfriend, who pushed and prodded until I invited her. I frowned and hoped Belle wouldn't make it to the island to attend the wedding. Maybe the ferry cancellations would keep her away.

I chewed on my lower lip. If she did show up, I hoped she'd behave herself and not make a scene, because I got the distinct impression she was angry at me for how I broke up with her and jumped into going out with Claire hours later. If she knew the truth, she'd be flaming angry with red-hot rage pouring out of her mouth. But she'll never find out what really happened.

12

CLAIRE

Driving on a paved two-lane road under a canopy of tree branches, I turned on the radio but only heard static. Rain drizzled down, and I flipped on the wipers. Going along winding Sills Road should have soothed me, but my gut churned with acid.

I braked and turned right on Dirt Road, following a lane that dipped down into a dark hollow. On my right, a chalet-style home squatted on an acre of land. On my left was the cute cottage Ralph rented for our honeymoon. He was crashing there with his best man after having the bachelor's party last night at a local bar on the island.

I frowned. Mack was a bad influence on Ralph and probably kept him up too late drinking. I turned left, and my tires crunched on a gravel driveway. I braked to a stop, turned off my car and jumped out. Every fiber of my being screamed how wrong this was for me to have to hunt down my fiancé on my wedding day.

I ran through the rain and trudged up the steps, rapping hard on the door with my knuckles. I was living a bride's nightmare, but I wouldn't put up with nonsense, not today. I hoped Mack hadn't talked him into staying out too late and, deep down, I was worried he'd turn into his drunken dad.

I cupped my hands, looking inside. Mack and Ralph slouched in armchairs. A set of French doors in the kitchen led out to a half-acre back yard. Grass by the house was mowed, but beyond that stood a wild, dark woods Tall trees swayed in the wind.

A man's voice grabbed my attention, singing a strange, melancholy tune, and I cocked my head to listen. Hidden in the woods, he sang about marriage, relationships and lost love. I nodded, because what he said made sense.

Hearing enough of the sad, eerie song, I shivered and hoped it wasn't an omen. I turned the door knob and barged inside to get our situation sorted out.

The cottage smelled like stale vomit, body odor and breath mints. The kitchen countertop was covered with crushed beer cans. Ralph and Mack were sprawled on easy chairs. I said, "We need to talk. Everything's falling apart."

Ralph stood, swaying back and forth. He clutched a hand to his stomach. "You're too loud. Talk in whispers. We're hungover."

"I gathered as much. How could you do this to me, on our wedding day? Don't you care?"

He winced and put an index finger to his lips. "Take it down a notch, will you? My head hurts."

Mack said, "Yeah, way too loud, considering how much we drank last night. We just woke up."

I glared at Ralph, shooting red-hot daggers at him, but he fell back in the chair and leaned over, putting his head in his hands. Did I really want to marry this man who was acting like an idiot? Maybe not.

13

MEG

The events manager breezed into the kitchen and said, "Meg, do you have a minute?"

Candy shifted on her feet, indicating something was wrong. I said, "Of course, what is it?"

She wrung her hands. "Did you know most of the wedding party and family are stuck on the Seattle side because the ferries are down?"

I threw a dishtowel at the sink and swore under my breath. Shaking my head, I said, "It's always something, isn't it? All the planning in the world goes down the drain, and we can't give them the perfect wedding they wanted."

She grew silent, and I said, "Wait, are you saying dinner will be delayed?"

She nodded. "I think so. The bride is thinking about it."

"How late are we talking about? Twenty minutes? If so, I can work with that."

She shook her head. "There's a small chance she'll want to move the dinner much later. I'm waiting to hear her decision, but I wanted to give you a heads up, just in case. Or, they might run on schedule and do the ceremony with very few people. It's her choice."

I said, "Thanks for letting me know. But I don't like it, not one bit."

"I figured you'd feel that way. I'll let you know what she decides as soon as I hear from her."

"Where is she? Maybe I can talk with her and help her decide."

Candy opened her hands and shrugged. "She left. She drove away, and I have no idea where she is."

Turning to my son and daughter, I said, "Now you can see how crazy this job is. Catering is not for sissies."

Troy laughed. "Franny and I are tough. We can handle it. Right, sis?"

She grinned and swatted him with a dishtowel. "Right."

I opened the fridge, letting cool air waft over me. This day was not working out how I pictured it. I didn't want to work late on a bride's whim because the ferries were three or four hours late. I deserved to get some rest tonight before hopping on the hamster treadmill tomorrow for the next big event.

Francesca came over. "Mom, what're you going to do if they want dinner served starting at ten tonight?"

I slammed the fridge door closed and sighed. "I'll try to talk them out of it."

14

CLAIRE

I threw my hands in the air and said, "Mack, would you please leave us alone for a few minutes?"

Mack rose and stumbled out of the room, heading toward the bathroom.

I sat in an armchair and leaned forward, searching Ralph's face for a glimpse of the man I had wanted to marry. The happy times we'd shared in this cottage near the beach came flooding back. One night, we played gin rummy and drank vodka gimlets, laughing so hard, my stomach hurt. But our moods shifted and soured when a neighbor knocked on the front door at ten at night, telling us we were too loud, which was weird.

Now, I said in a soft voice, "What's going on?"

Ralph winced. "I'm still drunk. I'm queasy and light-headed. We partied too hard last night."

I cocked my head. We were on an island, where most places closed early. I'd expected them to have a few beers and call it a night. "Did you go to Penny's?"

He barely nodded. "Yeah. We bought beers for the locals and shut the place down."

My eyebrows shot up, picturing the dim seen-better-days bar on Highway 20. It was short on charm but the only place open late on the south end of the island. Given how it was his big night to blow off steam before getting married, I softened my hard heart, but couldn't help saying, "Aren't you afraid of turning into your dad?"

He groaned. "Yeah, you know I am. I just went a bit overboard is all. But it doesn't change the fact that I want to marry you."

I nodded and reached over, patting his hand. "I'm superstitious, and we weren't supposed to see each other before the wedding, but we have a decision to make. That's why I drove down here."

He leaned back, closing his eyes. "We already made all the decisions. I'm glad that's over. What a huge hassle planning a wedding turned out to be. Who cares about the color of the napkins? I don't. And the cake, what a headache that was, finding a baker who'd make a cake in the shape of a tilting birch tree." He groaned.

I sprung out of my chair, sizzling with irritation at how we were on opposite sides of an emotional planet this afternoon. Pacing the floor, I felt like a parent to my future husband, by being the responsible one. I pointed a finger at him. "The ferries are running late, like by three hours, or maybe more. My dad and grandma and Rhonda and the bridesmaids will be three hours late, if we're lucky."

Ralph opened an eye. "Who was there with you at The Farm?"

I opened my hands. "No one. It's my wedding day, and I've been all alone, making sure everything looks right."

He waved a hand in front of his face. "No one cares about that. Only you do. Let it go. That's why they have an events manager on site."

I clenched my jaw. Our different outlooks on the world were grating on my nerves today. He was laid back and easy going, while I was more of a control freak, needing to make sure all was in order, down to the last detail. My hands-on tendency worked well in my career, but had been a fatal flaw in personal relationships. I was doing my best to throttle back on my needing to control every iota in my sphere of influence, but I was addicted to over-managing, after living in chaos growing up in a camper van, always moving around.

I cleared my throat. We were two flawed individuals about to tie the knot, and I intended to carry through and marry him. He put up with my foibles, and I'd return the favor. We just needed to keep laughing together.

Someone rapped hard on the front door, and I turned to see the pesky neighbor who came over one night when Ralph and I were playing cards and told us to tone it down. Going to the door, I glanced out at slanting rain pouring down, forming puddles on the dirt road.

I blew out a breath. I just had to make it through the next few hours. Then everything would fall into place, and my new life would begin.

15

DUKE

I paced back and forth in my living room, scowling and looking over gray water toward Port Townsend. I was fed up with tenants coming to the rental cottage down the lane and crowding out locals like us. I slapped a ball cap on my head and hurried through the rain to see my neighbor Ellen, who was also on the board of our Road Association.

Her house backed up to the woods, and she didn't have a water view, but she was a retired librarian and a rational person. I appreciated her sharp mind and valued her input. I rapped hard on her door and stared inside.

She set down her cup of tea and waved. coming to the door and opening it. "Duke, what can I do for you?"

"People at the cottage have three cars in the driveway, and one is sticking out, almost onto Dirt Road. We should've put it in the covenants that cars must be parked off the road by five feet or pay a fine."

She patted her short gray hair. "I'm sure they won't stay long. Don't worry about it."

I frowned. "I'll make a motion at the next Road Association meeting, and I hope you'll back me up."

"Fine, I'll do that."

I jabbed a finger in the air as rain drops pelted down. "We also need to add an amendment prohibiting short-term rentals. I'm fed up with people popping in for a few nights and driving off in a hurry, breaking the speed limit and ruining the road."

She sighed. "We've discussed the before. It's too late to stop the cottage owner from renting it out on a short-term basis. You've got to let it go."

I whooshed out a breath. "I'm not ready to do that. This was a peaceful place to live before the cottage was built and when the lot was vacant land. Now look what we have to deal with. People coming and going, increased traffic on the road, causing wear and tear that we'll have to pay to fix. This is a fight I won't give up."

"It's a losing battle, in my opinion."

My hands clenched. "We'll see about that. I'm going over there to talk to those short-timers who are invading our hollow."

"Don't be aggressive. We don't need the police down here again."

Rolling my eyes, I recalled the last time I threatened a

renter in the cottage. A young man with an inch of growth on his chin wore creased khaki pants and clean hiking boots, screaming city slicker. His flashy red convertible made me seethe with envy. When I spoke with him, he called the cops, who issued me a warning. Before I moved here, I was fired for hitting a patient in a Seattle emergency room. But that was ages ago, and I've learned to control my temper.

I shrugged. "I'll be my most charming self. See you later."

She closed the door, and I stomped down the lane past my house and took a right on Dirt Road, stomping over to the first house on my right. Tenants in the cottage slid and stomped down the steep trail to the beach we locals maintained without regard for the hours we put in installing rope handholds and clearing brush.

I smiled. During our last quarterly work party, I convinced the others to leave a patch of poison oak. We locals knew to avoid it going down to the beach, but the short-term renters had no idea. They'd itch and scratch and leave early, not coming back.

Distracted, I stepped in a puddle and swore. I'd emailed and called the cottage new owner, but she never got in touch with me. All I'd asked was for her to shutter the place as a rental and to give it to the Road Association for a club house. We'd use the land for a park. I'm not giving up on my great idea.

Stomping up the cottage steps, I glared at the three

parked cars. While I waited for someone to come to the door, I screwed up my face. Maybe I'd been a bit too hard on the old man that bought the land and built the cottage. After one of my run-ins with him, he collapsed on this very front porch and died from a fatal heart attack. But it wasn't my fault. He shouldn't have gotten so upset at my suggestion that he clear out and go back to the city and give us his place.

16

RALPH

A man in his late forties in a black and white flannel shirt rapped on the door of the cottage. Claire marched over to it, and I stood, swaying back and forth. Clutching my stomach, I did my best to dampen my drunken stupor.

In a weak voice, I said, "Don't let him in. I don't want to talk to him."

But I spoke too late. She opened the door and said to the stranger, "Hello, can I help you?"

I moaned. The hangover made my mind muddy and slow.

She turned to me. "What did you say?"

The man stepped inside, tugging on his blue ball cap. Everything about him signaled he was ready for a fight. His hands were fisted, his face flushed, and his dark flat eyes narrowed. He stabbed an index finger in my direction and said in a loud voice, "You, you're the problem. I've seen you here in the hollow before, ruining our road. Why don't you go back to the city where you belong?"

My skin itched, and I scratched my wrist, where red bumpy welts were forming. Time slid past, but I didn't have it in me to wrestle verbally with this weird stranger, not today, not on my wedding day, not when my head hurt.

The man grinned, studying my wrist. "Bet you got a case of poison oak, don't you? Too bad you used our private trail down to the beach. That'll teach you not to take advantage of what we maintain. And you drive too fast. The speed limit is ten miles an hour, but I've seen you flying down the hill at thirty, creating ruts in the road."

I took a breath and gathered my strength to fight, but the seething man continued before I could utter a word.

He said, "You have no idea what it takes to maintain the road. We share the costs to maintain it, but people renting this home use it far more than locals do. It's not fair, and I intend to do something about it."

Claire crossed her arms and glanced at the road. My future wife avoids conflict, so this toxic neighbor had to be upsetting her.

My head throbbed, but I spoke up. "Don't worry about it. We'll be spending our honeymoon here and not leaving the house. Your precious road will be safe from us."

Mack lumbered into the living room. "But I'll be here for the week."

I cocked my head. "You're not staying here. We are. We booked it for our honeymoon. It's a special place for us."

Mack smiled. "I'll run my podcast out of here, tuning in from Barnacle Island. It'll be great."

I shook my head. My best friend was a known moocher, and I'd fallen into his trap before. "Mack, three's a crowd. No way you're staying here."

The invader in a checked black and white flannel shirt scowled. Pointing at Mack, he said, "There's no internet down here in the hollow. It's a dark spot on the island. So, good luck with that."

Mack sighed, running a hand through his hair. "Maybe I'll reconsider my plans and move on after the wedding."

I straightened up to my full height of five-foot nine and said to the local jerk, "We're getting married today, and I'd appreciate it if you left the premises. We have some decisions to make."

The angry man looked from Mack to me. "You're getting married?"

I moved over to Claire, slipping an arm over her shoulder. "Claire and I are getting married at The Farm. We picked it because we have fond memories of staying here at the cottage on Barnacle Island."

I gave Claire a peck on the cheek, and she winced. My breath must be bad enough to melt paint off a car. I let go of Claire and moved to the door, scratching my itching wrist. "So, if that's all, we've got to say goodbye to you. We have a wedding to go to, before it's too late."

The man snorted. "Good luck with that today. The ferries are running late. And while I'm at it, move that car from the road. It's sticking out and creating a traffic hazard."

Claire put her hands on her hips. "That's mine, and I'll be leaving soon. We have to say goodbye to you now, because we have serious issues to discuss."

She opened the door and motioned for the local guy to leave. He sent me a final glare, tugged on the brim of his blue ball cap and stomped down the steps, heading through the rain toward a house on the bluff.

Closing the door, Claire frowned. "We have to make some quick decisions. If we go ahead with the ceremony, we'll miss most of our guests. And what about dinner? By the time people get here, assuming the ferry is fixed, it'll be too late to serve them dinner."

I went over and gave her a hug. She sobbed into my shoulder and wailed, "I wanted everything to be perfect, but it's all wrong. What're we going to do? And Cousin Lacey showed up, just to make things worse."

I pulled away. "Your cousin Lacey is here? You saw her?"

Claire wiped her eyes. "Yes, she was creeping around The Farm, like she was planning something. She's wearing a cloak with a hood and carrying a big slingshot."

Mack cleared his throat. "She sounds interesting. I'd

like to meet this Lacey. She might be a good guest on my podcast."

I winced at how podcast-centric he was and how everything was all about him. Chewing on the inside of my cheek, my mind flashed to the threatening cards Lacey sent my future bride. I wasn't going to let a redheaded cousin wreck our wedding. I'd already done enough damage to Claire's day by being drunk in the afternoon of our big day.

I said to Mack, "Give the podcast a break for today. We've got real problems on our hands."

Claire tapped her chin. "Wait, Mack's idea could work. He could distract Lacey and stop her from sabotaging our wedding and reception."

I nodded and went in the kitchen, taking a jug of water from the fridge. Well water at the cottage was rusty-brown most of the time. Disgusting was the word and undrinkable. Pouring three glasses of bottled water, I handed one to Claire and Mack, who chugged it down.

Taking a sip, I said, "You're right. That'd work. Mack are you up for it? She's a redheaded fire ball with a temper. She's angry she wasn't picked for best bride's maid or whatever you call it."

"Maid of honor," Claire said. "Or, just a bride's maid."

Mack shrugged and grinned. "You can count on me to protect you on your wedding day. That's what I'm supposed to do."

Claire drank the water and set down her glass on the

kitchen counter. "I have to tell the events manager what time we'll hold the ceremony and if we'll delay dinner or go ahead with just a few people."

Mack chuckled. "You mean basically a ceremony and dinner for just your cousin Lacey, me and you two? That sounds weird, but I guess it could work."

Thoughts raced through my mind, and I latched onto an idea. I smiled and said, "How about this?"

17

CLAIRE

I ran to my car and jumped in, driving down the dirt road at the mandated ten miles an hour until I turned left onto Sills Road, heading for The Farm. A mile from the hollow, where grumpy neighbors lingered and loomed, my phone dinged, and dinged again. I glanced at the device but kept driving. I didn't have time to talk with my friends or father. I needed to deliver our decision to the events manager and get things rolling in a new direction.

Rain drummed down on my car, and the road was slick, so I slowed down. Today was not the day to end up in a ditch and wait for a tow truck. I cringed, imagining more disasters afoot and picturing my car running off the road and rolling over in an area where I didn't have cell reception.

Shaking my head, I banished the flights of dark fancy

and pulled into a parking spot at The Farm marked "Bride to Be."

I jumped out, slammed the car door and hurried to the office. My wedding plans were out the window. Nothing was the way I wanted it. But it would be a fine event anyway. I just had to adjust my mindset and get ready.

Striding down a hall, I looked around for my cousin, who might be lurking somewhere, plotting my downfall. I'd stay on the lookout for Cousin Lacey trying to pull a fast one and ruin my wedding over a perceived slight.

18

CANDY, EVENTS MANAGER

The bride marched into my office, resting her hands on her hips. "Do you have a minute?"

I closed my laptop and stood, gesturing to a chair. "Of course. Won't you sit down?"

She glanced out the window and shook her head. "I've got a lot to do to get ready, and this won't take long. Have you seen the woman we saw outside with red hair? She was wearing a hooded cape and carrying a sling shot?"

I released a slow breath. Claire was more relaxed than she'd been when she left, almost as if she'd had a moment of enlightenment and she was taking things in stride. This was a boon and a huge benefit for me, because weddings were tough enough without our having a nervous bride hovering and worrying over every last detail. I hoped what I was about to tell her wouldn't send her into a tail spin of angst.

I opened my hands and said, "I'm sorry to tell you this, but your Cousin Lacey is here. She came inside and is sitting by the fire having a coffee at this very moment, out by the stone fireplace. Her coat was wet, so I had someone hang it up and give her a warm blanket."

I expected Claire to fuss and fume, but she shrugged and said, "Okay, that's great. Here's our plan."

I grabbed a pen and pad of paper, jotting down notes and nodding. It was an odd approach but fitted the circumstances. "That's good. We can make it work."

She gave me a smile and waved, walking away.

19

MEG

Bending over a stainless mixing bowl, I stirred the blue cheese dressing I'd made, using my secret recipe. Chunks of blue-veined cheese stood out, and I glanced over, smiling at my two grown children. It was a comfort to have Francesca and Troy helping me cater the event, and I enjoyed having them around, despite my doubts about my daughter fitting in. But so far, she was working hard, washing pots and pans at the sink.

The bride appeared and cleared her throat. "Hi, sorry to bother you, but could I please get a cup of coffee?"

My eyebrows shot up, because not long ago, I saw her run out in the rain to her car and drive away. But here she was, with messy brown hair, looking relaxed and at ease. Something must have happened while she was gone. I'll ask Candy what decision was made about the timing for dinner. I'd rather Candy be the go between and buffer, so I won't ask Claire. She has enough on her mind.

I set the spoon in the metal mixing bowl, and it clanked against the side. "Yes, we'd be happy to do that for you."

She smiled, showing brilliant white teeth. "That'd be great."

I turned to my son. "Troy, will you get Claire a cup of coffee, please?"

From her position at the sink, Francesca wiped her face on her sleeve. "I can do it."

Recalling how she could sometimes be clumsy, I said, "Thanks, but Troy will do it. I need you washing dishes. You're doing a great job."

To the bride, I said, "Would you like something to eat? You must be famished."

She beamed. "What do you have? I'm starving."

I reeled off choices, counting on my fingers. "I can make a cheese plate with crackers, gluten-free if you'd like, or a charcuterie board with sliced meat, or a hummus platter."

She tapped a finger to her gorgeous full lips. I swallowed with envy, recalling when estrogen coursed through my body, making my skin glow. I'd been young once and a bride, but time had marched on, leaving me a shell of the woman I was in appearance, but wiser from life's lessons.

Claire said, "It may sound strange, but what I'd really

like is two scrambled eggs and a piece of toast. Can you do that? I'm sorry to impose when you're so busy."

I grinned. I'd bet the poor girl was withering into nothing, almost evaporating before my eyes from a rigid pre-wedding diet. I'd seen it many times. Last week, a bride fainted during her wedding ceremony. And then we've had drunk grooms who imbibed too much the night before. One passed out twice before saying his vows, so they propped him up in a chair, and he keeled over, falling on the floor. Oh, the stories we could tell.

"Yes, I'd love to do that for you. Is it all right if I use butter?"

She said, "Slather it on. After the day I've had, I want to ditch the diet. I could eat the entire birch tree cake all by myself."

Her stomach growled, and she covered her mouth, giggling. Troy handed her a large mug of black coffee, saying, "Do you take cream or sugar or artificial sweetener?"

She shook her head. "No, thanks. This is all I need for now. Why don't you make the eggs and toast for two of us and bring it out to the fireplace? I'll be sitting with my cousin. If she's still there, that is."

She walked away holding the mug, and when she turned the corner and was out of hearing range, I said to Francesca and Troy, "Sounds mysterious, what's going on. I'll check with Candy to see how the schedule looks and when dinner will be served."

20

FRANCESCA

I wiped my sweating brow on my sleeve and let out a sigh. Catering and helping in the kitchen was far more work than I'd anticipated. Mom and I practiced me carrying plates with food and bowls of soup last night, but there's far more involved, like scrubbing pots and pans, than I imagined when I took this job.

When the bride asked for a cup of coffee, I spoke up, wanting to help. "I'll get that."

But a flash of fear crossed Mom's face before she wiped it away. She said, "Keep washing dishes. I need you doing that. You brother can get it."

I went back to scrubbing a huge frying pan that weighed ten tons. My wrists ached. My shoulders were tight. I turned off the water and stretched for a minute, wondering if I'd ever be a bride one day, walking down the aisle. I tried to picture my estranged father walking me down the aisle but shook my head. I hadn't seen him in years, since we visited and he took my brother and me to Rodeo Beach near Mill Valley in California. But that was many years ago, and we rarely spoke.

The bride asked for scrambled eggs and toast, and I smiled. My stomach gurgled. I'd skipped breakfast and lunch to get here on time.

When the bride marched away, carrying her mug of coffee like it was a well-won prize, I sidled up to my mother. 'Would you make me some eggs too? I'm hungry."

Mom frowned. "Did you eat anything today?"

"No, I was in a hurry and didn't have time."

She shook a finger at me. "You can't run on empty in this job. You've got to put fuel in the tank to have the stamina needed to work in catering."

I cringed. Mom's work was daunting, and I doubted I wanted to join her long-term. A job in the garden store was looking better than ever, although my catering gig had barely begun.

She said, "Fine, I'll whip up the bride's food, and then make you and your brother some, if he wants."

Troy said, "Yes, please. I'm starving."

I smiled. "Thanks, Mom, you make the best scrambled eggs. I'll get back to washing dishes."

While I scrubbed bowls at the sink, Troy took two plates of toast and eggs to the bride.

He came back in the kitchen and tapped my shoulder, saying in a low voice, "There's some weird family dynamics going on by the fireplace now. It's like the bride and her cousin haven't seen each other in forever, but they're arch enemies."

My eyebrows shot up, and I turned off the water, wiping my hands on a towel. "We know about strange family dynamics. We're experts and could write a book on the topic."

Mom called out from the stove, where she was cooking scrambling eggs, "What're you two talking about?"

Troy shrugged. "Weird families, like ours."

Mom cocked her head. "What do you mean? We're normal, like everybody else."

I laughed. "Come on, Mom. Dad lives in an apartment, which his mother owns, and he rarely leaves and doesn't work. And the fact that he walked out on us is anything but normal."

Troy nodded. "And Grandma, his mom, is cold as an icicle."

Mom shrugged. "You two win, and I guess we do have an odd family. Get your bread or toast, because the eggs are ready."

I said, "Thanks."

"You're welcome. Now get a move on. We have a lot to do before the wedding."

The three of us sat hunched over on barstools in the kitchen, eating the best eggs in the world. I groaned with my mouth full, chewing. The eggs tasted of salt and pepper, a hint of cayenne, fresh chopped parsley, creamy butter and a dash of milk. Soon, our plates were clean, and my belly was full. All I had to do was get through this event and look for other work. Now that I was here, I realized it wasn't a good fit. Mom would understand if I quit. I was sure of it.

21

TROY

I gathered Mom's and Franny's plates and placed them in the dishwasher along with mine. "That was delicious. Okay, what's next? What would you like me to do?

Mom said, "I'll go talk with the events manager about the program. Troy, why don't you check on Claire and her cousin? See if they've finished eating and if they'd like a croissant or anything else."

Franny frowned. "What about me? What should I do?"

Mom pointed to the sink. "Keep washing dishes, dear. There's still a stack for you to tackle."

Franny said, "Why does he get to do the fun jobs, and I have to wash dishes?"

Mom said, "Because he's helped me before, and you haven't. He knows what he's doing in the kitchen, and he's good with customers."

Franny pouted. 'Are you saying I'm not?"

Mom threw up her hands. "Listen, enough of this. I'll be right back."

22

COUSIN LACEY

Pulling a blanket tight around my shoulders, I shivered by a blazing fire on a rainy afternoon. I'd come here intending to ruin my cousin's wedding, but no one else was around. My cloak was sopping wet, but a staff member took it to hang up and dry.

I sighed, playing with a strand of hair and wiggling my wet toes. I left home with a half-cocked idea of sending rocks zinging past Claire's head with my slingshot before she took her vows. I toyed with the idea of shooting paint balls at the bride and her maid of honor and bridesmaids. Right now, as rain drummed down on the roof, the paint-ball attack carried allure, but I'd been too lazy to arrange it.

Gazing into the crackling fire, I screwed up my face.

The Farm was basically empty, with only few people around before the wedding. I watched Claire run out into the rain a little while ago, sprinting for her car, but then she came roaring back. She's alone on her wedding day, without family or friends, which must be a bummer. I'm almost starting to feel sorry for her.

A smile spread across my face, thinking of how I managed to locate Claire's missing no-good mother, who left Claire when she was a girl. I was so angry Claire didn't pick me to be in her bridal party that I wanted revenge, and the best way I knew to ruin her wedding was to dredge up her long-gone Mom. Just wait until Kendra shows up. Won't that be a surprise.

I flinched when my cousin Claire came into the room carrying a mug of coffee. I didn't expect to see her in the public area wearing street clothes. She had a bride's glow about her, with rosy cheeks.

Claire said, "Hey, okay if I sit with you? I could use the company. No one else is around."

I gestured to a brown leather armchair. "Sure. Bummer, right? The ferry problems are ruining your wedding plans."

Claire sipped her coffee and gazed at the fire. "I'm learning a lot today about letting go and enjoying what happens. This is the craziest wedding I've ever attended, and it definitely is not going according to plan."

She shrugged and went on. "But it doesn't really

matter, does it, how I feel? Because no matter how hard I've tried to wrestle this wedding into submission, every iota is spinning out of control. The cake was sliding, for one thing. Did you see it yet?"

I nodded and didn't mention I ran my finger through the icing along the side and took a taste. "It looks delicious."

"It almost fell on the floor, and it's my fault. I insisted on having a tilting wedding cake with a branch sticking out. I thought I knew better than the baker, but it turns out I didn't."

I suppressed a grin, secretly pleased she was suffering today. I'd harbored a great green jealousy seething inside for years about how her father fawned on her and drove her around the country, while I was stuck in a small town. She moved to the city and climbed the corporate ladder, while I was a waitress, living on measly tips. She met someone and was getting married. I was single and people I knew from high school were all married by now, except for me. It wasn't fair, none of it, and I figured this was my time to get back at her for having a better life, where everything was easy.

She said, "Did you know my dad and grandmother are stuck on the Seattle side? And the entire bridal party."

I sniffed, irritated at her mentioning the stupid bridal party, a vestige from the past. Although I looked down on her hoity-toity wedding with all the bells and whistles, I desperately wanted to be needed, wanted and included in the idiotic event.

My throat was dry, and I took a slug of coffee, swallowing the bitter brew. Staring at the fire, I said, "That's your maternal grandmother?"

"Yeah."

I said, "But what about your mom? Where is she these days?"

Claire's face turned pale, and her lower lip trembled. "I don't know, and I never want to see her again. She's not welcome here today, or in my life. Leaving like she did is an unforgiveable act."

A good-looking guy with short sandy hair wearing a green apron came over to us, offering us plates with scrambled eggs, toast and jam. My mouth watered.

Claire took a plate and said, "Thank you." Looking at me, she said, "Are you hungry? I had them make enough for you."

I hesitated, because what I had planned for later today possibly fell in the unforgivable category, but it was too late to stop the train from rolling now. What I'd set in motion months ago was happening, whether I liked it or not, when I was almost having a change of heart.

I bit my lip. Kendra, Claire's mother, was coming, and her appearance would cause chaos, leaving the wedding in shambles. But I wouldn't breathe a word. I was hungry and tired from traveling to the island last night and camping in a forest. We'd see how it played out. Kendra was a flake, so she might not show up anyway.

"Sure," I said, taking the plate and inhaling aromas of chopped chives, fresh butter and sharp cheddar cheese, "I'm starving. Let's eat."

The server handed us silverware rolled in yellow cloth napkins and said, "I'll refill your coffees, be right back."

As he walked off, I said in a low voice, "I'll take one of him too, while I'm at it."

Claire giggled, covering her mouth. "He's not for you. He gives off commitment phobia vibes. I'm an expert at that, and I could read the signals a mile off."

I nodded. "Just another lonely soul wandering the planet, meant to be alone."

I bit into a buttered triangle of toast and moaned. Chewing and swallowing, I said, "How can toast taste this good?"

She shoveled a forkful of eggs into her mouth, hunching over and looking like she hadn't eaten for days. Pointing to her plate, she said with her mouth full, "Try the eggs. They're amazing."

For the next ten minutes, we sat beside each other eating breakfast and sipping fresh hot coffee by the fire. But an inner clock of guilt ticked within me. The wedding was coming up, when everything I'd planned would rain down.

I handed my plate to the kitchen guy and leaned back

in the chair. I snorted when Claire said she told her dad to buy a nose hair trimmer before the wedding. If he didn't, she wouldn't let him walk her down the aisle.

We chuckled, leaning back in our chairs. A wave of regret washed over me, and I sighed, regretting what I'd set in motion. But it was too late to call it off now.

23

RALPH, THE GROOM

I waved goodbye to Claire and closed the door, turning to my best man Mack. "I'll jump in the shower and then you can take one."

He shrugged. "Sorry, buddy, but I used up the hot water."

I cocked my head. "I wish you hadn't done that, today of all days."

He opened his hands. "When you and Claire were talking, I took a shower. But the water is weird here. It's rusty-brown, and I felt like I couldn't get clean."

My wrists and hands itched, and I clenched my jaw, resisting the urge to scratch my skin raw. I must've brushed up against poison oak plants on the way down to the beach yesterday before we went out for too many beers.

I gazed out a window at a dreary gray rainy day,

mulling over regrets. I didn't tell Claire I'd invited my ex-girlfriend to the wedding, and she was due to show up any minute. Everyone loved Belle. She was all smiles and the most interesting person, but we parted ways after fighting about money too often. She bought the best of the best and went deep into debt, while I spent as little as I could and paid off my credit cards each month. I realized the relationship was destined to fail one evening when we were at a fancy restaurant she'd picked. She ordered the most expensive thing on the menu, a huge steak, and a pricey bottle of wine for herself, which she always did. I squirmed in my seat, thinking of the bill, and stuck to fish and chips and water.

She ordered dessert and dug into a parfait glass of chocolate mousse, but set her spoon down after taking one bite and said, "I'm finished."

I cleared my throat and leaned in. "I'm sorry, but I'm finished too."

She dabbed at her lips and squinted at me. "What do you mean?"

I sighed. "I can't do this anymore. We're too different."

Her mouth dropped open. "We watch the same shows and laugh at the same lines."

"That's not enough. I'm sorry, but I think one of us needs to find a new place to live, starting tomorrow."

She glared. "You're the one moving out, starting tonight."

We went into the restaurant as lovers and left as roommates running away from each other toward separate lives. That night, I spent the night at Mack's, and the next day I saw Claire at a coffee shop. I was attracted to her confident manner and how easy it was to talk with her, and the rest is history.

A flicker of guilt flitted past, and I chewed on the inside of my cheek, because there was more to the story than what I'd told Belle at the restaurant that night when I broke it off.

I scratched at my wrists and the back of my hands. Claire and Belle hadn't met, and I intended to keep them apart at the wedding reception. We didn't need sparks of jealousy over my secret past to erupt at the reception. I meant to mention Belle to Claire, but the timing never felt right, and after a while, it was too late to bring up the subject.

I turned to Mack. "I'll take a cold shower. But I have a job for you. I want you during the wedding and reception to keep Claire from meeting Belle. Can you do that?"

He pulled his long brown hair back in a man bun. I wasn't a fan of that look, but I didn't give him grooming tips. It was far too late for that. I pressed my lips together and waited.

Mack shook his head. "That won't work, because I'll have my hands full with Cousin Lacey. You dug your grave, buddy, and you're on your own."

I groaned. "Come on, do your best. That's all I ask."

He shrugged. "I'll try, but I can't guarantee they won't

meet. Maybe it'll be no big deal. Why did you invite Belle anyway, if you're nervous about her being there?"

I sighed. "I felt bad that I broke it off with her right before she took the CPA exam. My timing wasn't the best, and I should've waited a few weeks or months. I've always suspected she failed the exam and had to retake it because of me."

Mack laughed. "Get over yourself. No one's that important. She passed eventually, right?"

"She did. But she called last year and asked if I was going out with anyone. I mentioned I was getting married, and she basically invited herself to the wedding. I couldn't get out of it."

Mack stared at me. "Get a spine, or people will walk all over you."

I made a face, knowing Mack was right, but I didn't have time to think about it. "I'll hop in the shower, and we'll get dressed and head out."

But as I marched down the hall toward my future, an unpleasant thought wound its way through my mind. In many ways, I was marrying a woman very much like Belle. Claire liked to spend money, and when she picked the venue for our wedding, she spared no expense. I wanted to get married at City Hall, but she got her way by saying it was her special day. I'd caved and agreed to everything she wanted, figuring it was a once-in-a-lifetime event, but the costs were creeping into the stratosphere, equal to making a down payment on a house.

I rested a hand on my churning gut. The thought of the credit card charges racking up was enough to make me feel sick. In the bathroom, I took off my clothes and turned on the shower. Chilly rusty-brown water sprayed out, and I stepped in.

A shiver ran up my spine, and goose bumps pricked my flesh. A feeling of foreboding swept over me, but I shrugged it off and scrubbed with soap. My skin felt slippery, slick and not at all clean. We'd had our share of bad luck so far today, with ferry cancellations, and we were due for a change and a much better day. Claire deserved her happy wedding, after our paying so much for the event.

Turning off the water, I stepped out and toweled off with a dark brown fluffy towel. An ugly stray thought flit through my distracted mind, and I frowned, swatting it away. What if I was making a mistake by marrying Claire? What if there was someone out there who was even better for me? I went right from a relationship with Belle into seeing Claire. Maybe I wasn't seeing things clearly.

I hung up my towel and picked up Mack's bath towel from the floor. I'd been in a hurry to move out of his place back then after the Belle break up and escape how messy he was. I hope I didn't make a mistake by diving in too soon with Claire.

24

BELLE

Driving north on I-5 from Seattle, I turned off and headed west on Highway 20, going past refineries on my right with white plumes coming out of many tall smokestacks. I continued on and went past a small lake, going through a forest. Crossing over the Deception Pass Bridge, I glanced to my right and looked out over gray choppy water. Down below, whirlpools of strong currents swirled, and people stood on a sandy beach, fishing from the shoreline.

Rain pattered down on the windshield, and I hunched over, gripping the wheel and taking slow breaths to calm myself. I'd dropped a dress size for the event, had my nails and hair done, with the ultimate goal of outshining the bride and making Ralph regret dumping me that night at the restaurant.

I shook my head. I mean, who tells someone they're

leaving them at a restaurant, of all places? In public is the worst, cruel way to cut someone off.

I swallowed hard. When he said he was finished, I acted like it was no big deal, but my heart was utterly broken. My pulse raced, and my hands clenched under the table. My fingernails cut into my palms. I was ready to knock him down flat, but I acted cavalier, so as not to make a scene. I've dreamed of ways to get back at him for his cowardly, casual way of dumping me. I couldn't believe it when he acted like ending our love was no big deal.

I drove past a Naval Air Station and tipped back my head, letting out a loud laugh. I'd finagled an invitation to the wedding for the sole purpose of rubbing Ralph's nose in his huge mistake. He hurt me and didn't care. But by the time this day was over, he'd deeply regret jilting me. I was going to finally make him pay.

Driving south on Highway 20, I noticed a thrift store but shook my head. I didn't have time to shop. I wanted to get to The Farm to foment disaster. The morning after he ditched me cruelly at the restaurant, I wandered past a coffee shop and stopped to stare.

My mouth dropped open, and I gazed through the window glass. Ralph smiled and looked into Claire's eyes, and she touched his arm, laughing at something he said. Ever since then, I've hunted for ways to burst their happy bubble, and I've finally come up with a well-crafted plan.

I nodded to myself. For all I knew, they were going out before he left me. Clenching my jaw, I pictured the wedding reception. I'd flirt with Ralph and make sure Claire saw it. She'll seethe with jealousy and storm off. The wedding couple will fight on their wedding night, perhaps right in public. That will spell success. And I have more ways up my sleeves for how I'll wreck this wedding and create a nightmare. By the time I'm through, they'll regret getting together. Someone's going to die today, if my plans go through. No one dumps me and lives to tell the tale.

25

CLAIRE

The server took our plates and asked if we wanted more coffee. My cousin Lacey and I shook our heads at the same time, and I noticed she had my Dad's strong beak-like nose. As the waiter left, I leaned over and said, "Hey, I wanted to ask you something."

Lacey rolled her eyes. "Okay, fine, what is it?"

I patted her hand. "Would you be my maid of honor?"

Her jaw dropped. "You're asking me now but not before? Just because no one else showed up but your cousin, who went to a lot of trouble to get here on time, not like the others. My feelings were hurt, you know. I'm not leftovers or a last resort."

I nodded. "I realize that, and I didn't mean to hurt your feelings. It was just easier, because Rhonda and the others live in Seattle, to get together and talk over plans."

Lacey sniffed, wiping her nose with the back of her hand. "We could've talked on the phone. That's a lame excuse. I'm not sure I want to help you out after what you did, giving me the cold shoulder."

I stood, flashing a smile. I probably looked like a lunatic, standing in jeans before my wedding and grinning, but I wanted to bring her over to my side and mend the family rift I'd created. Good grief, putting on a wedding was a big pain, far more than I'd realized. Maybe Ralph's idea of going to the courthouse wasn't such a bad idea. It was my fault for picking this venue on an island and holding it on a busy summer weekend.

In my kindest voice, I said, "Lacey, will you be my maid of honor? I'd love it if you'd help me out."

She studied the ceiling. "If I don't say yes, what'll you do?"

I sighed. "I guess I'll do without. Come on, help a girl out."

I held out my hand, and she took it, standing with a half-smile.

She threw off her blanket, tossing it on the chair. "What'd you need? Tell me what to do, and I'll do it."

I picked up the blanket and folded it, setting it down. "I need to get into my dress, and my hair's a mess. Did you bring anything else to wear?"

She shrugged. "Nope, this is me. Nothing special, but with a big heart."

I patted her shoulder. "You look beautiful, just the way you are. Come on, let's go. We don't have much time."

26

KENDRA, CLAIRE'S MOTHER

When I saw on the news that the ferries were short-staffed and one boat was temporarily out of service with mechanical problems, I set my mind to the problem. My daughter was getting married today on Barnacle Island, according to her cousin who contacted me. I absolutely had to get there on time.

Going online, I searched for alternative ways to the island. On a lark, I called a seaplane company and learned they'd take me from South Lake Union in Seattle to the island for a handsome fee. After that, I'd rely on a driver to take me to The Farm. It would cost a fair amount, but it'd be worth it. We'd been apart for far too many years.

I smiled and was sure Claire would be happy to see me. Mother and daughter would be reunited at the wedding. It should be sweet, but for years, I'd plotted to get back at her father for leaving me in Grays Harbor. He took off in the camper van, and I woke up in the tent, rubbing my head. He'd put a sleeping pill in my wine and took off with our daughter. I tried to track Claire down, but he was always on the move, hiding from me, evading my efforts to pin them down. I couldn't tell the police because we were wanted by the law for holding up a bank with a cap gun, back before Claire was born. But then we went straight, for our daughter's sake.

I climbed out of a car by Lake Union, waved to the driver and strode down wooden dock planks to a waiting seaplane. Rain pattered down, getting my hair wet, but I didn't care. I'd fix it when I got to The Farm.

I grinned. Soon, I'd hug my daughter and drug the jerk of her father with his own drink tonight. He could suffer for all I cared after hiding her for so long and changing her first name, according to Cousin Lacey, from Tasha to Claire, and her last name to Cleveland. I'll never forgive him for that. He kept us apart for too long, but that's about to change. He'll be the odd man out, wishing he were dead by the time I'm done with him.

I nodded to the pilot and stepped onboard the seaplane, buckling up my seatbelt. I didn't have luggage because I travel light, ready to take flight. I'm a come as you are kind of person, take me or leave me. Maybe at The Farm I can borrow a sparkling barrette or necklace for the ceremony and reception.

The plane engine rumbled and whined. Taxiing over

the water and taking flight, we soared over yachts, houseboats and kayakers. Rain smeared the side windows, and I rested a hand on my growling stomach. My life was about to take off, like this small winged seaplane, just the way I'd hoped it would. Everything would change for me on Barnacle Island.

27

MACK, THE BEST MAN

I helped Ralph put on his black tuxedo jacket and stepped back, grinning. "Looks great, man. Claire's going to be proud to be marrying you."

Ralph scratched his wrist, where red welts formed. I slapped his arm and said, "Cut that out, or you'll be oozing in no time. You don't want to gross her out at the altar, do you?"

He cringed and thrust his hands into his armpits. "Good point. I'll stop. We should stop and buy calamine lotion along the way."

I wrinkled my nose. "That stuff has an odor. Just skip it. You'll be fine."

A flicker of concern crossed his face. "I hope I'm doing the right thing."

I clapped a hand on his shoulder. "What're you talking about? Of course you are. She's perfect for you."

He tapped a finger to his lips. "I hope so."

"Come on, let's go. Time's wasting." I took the car keys from him and said, "Best man drives. No arguments."

Rain pelted the windows, and puddles formed on the dirt road out front. We pulled on rain jackets over our tuxedos and hurried out in the rain to the car.

28

MEG

A metal bowl clattered, dropping with a crash and clang onto the kitchen floor. I made my way from the bathroom and studied my workspace, where my two grown kids were helping out. Sure, enough, as I suspected, Francesca bent by the sink, picking up a bowl. She took out a dish towel, wiped off the bowl with a split-second stroke and set it on the counter.

I shook my head and went over to her. "Hon, you know that isn't clean. It hit the floor. Wash it again. We don't take shortcuts here, especially not with our guests' health."

Her eyes grew wide. "Sorry, Mom. I'll do better."

I drew her into a hug, patting her back. My daughter was tender with deep feelings, which was a burden for her to shoulder on her own. Her brother and I made sure to stay in her orbit and see each other often to keep

Francesca from feeling low. Christmas Eve was a particularly troubling time for us, because it brought back traumatic memories of being left. No one likes being abandoned, and my kids and I unfortunately had that in common.

I stepped back, gazing into her eyes. "You can do this job. I know you can. All you have to do is focus."

She shrugged. "I'll try. Now I've got to get back to washing dishes."

She wiped a tear from her eye and turned her back on me, washing the errant stainless steel mixing bowl. I'd have to keep a close watch on my girl to make sure she didn't sink too low. Weddings can do that to some people and bring them down, making the odd woman out feel even more isolated and alone in the aftermath of a joyous event.

I caught Troy's gaze and nodded to him. We'd watch over Francesca and make sure she was surrounded by love. I'll protect my children with my dying breath. In rare calls with their estranged father, he yammered on about them being rich when he passed away. I bet the kids would rather feel loved by their dad than rolling in dough at a later date, but he just was too short-sighted to realize it.

29

COUSIN LACEY

Claire led me down a hall, where dark wood floors gleamed, and wall scones emitted soft light. We turned the corner and our footsteps were muffled as we made our way along a red woven runner. She paused at a carved wooden door, tapped a keycard against a device, and the lock clicked.

Claire swung open the door and stepped inside. I stood at the threshold, gaping at the elegant room. I'd never been in one as fancy as this.

Claire turned on a gas fireplace, and flames flickered, dancing for her special day. A couch and wingchairs beckoned by the fire. Brass light fixtures gleamed.

I stepped inside and scanned the room. Small wrapped chocolates filled a bowl on a wood vanity with a mirror on the wall. A large standing gold-framed mirror reflected light.

Claire peered out leaded glass windows at a flower garden, and I joined her. Slanted rain poured down, and daisies swayed in a steady breeze. This was definitely not a day to hold a wedding outside.

Gazing around the room, I swallowed hard, realizing I had no place being here helping my cousin. I was just a waitress from a small town. This is so far beyond what I'm accustomed to, I might as well be on Mars. I should go home, where I belong.

My hands clenched, and my armpits pricked with sweat. I pivoted in place and rushed to the door. With a trembling hand on the door handle, I said to Claire, "You were probably right not to pick me. I have no idea what I'm doing, and I don't know how to help you."

She glided over, resting a cool hand on mine. "You don't need to do anything special. Just stay and hang out with me. That's what I need right now."

I swallowed tears, stemming from a case of jealousy over her success, and shook my head. "I'm so sorry, I shouldn't have planned to ruin your wedding."

Her eyes opened wide, and she stepped back. "What do you mean you planned to ruin my wedding? What did you do?"

30

CANDY

I pressed my lips together and took a deep breath before striding into the kitchen to talk with Meg. I knew she wouldn't be happy about the news I was about to deliver. But the show must go on, and the bride is always right.

Pausing in the entry for a moment, I watched Meg and her two grown kids working in the kitchen. The daughter scrubbed pans at the sink. Her son chopped vegetables, and Meg stirred a vat of butternut squash soup.

I sighed, wishing I had as positive a relationship with my daughter as Meg had with her children. I've tried for years but can't get my daughter Cara to call me back. Maybe I shouldn't have moved so far from her to take this job when she was in high school.

I said, "Meg, can I talk with you for a minute?"

She set down the ladle and came over, wiping her

hands on a green apron with The Farm logo in black ink. "What's up? Did you hear from the bride about when she'd like dinner served?"

I patted her shoulder. "I did. Here's the plan."

I reviewed the schedule, and Meg frowned, putting her hands on her hips.

She shook her head. "That's highly unusual, and I'm not sure I like it."

I said, "But you can do it, right? No problem?"

Meg nodded. "We'll be ready. Thanks for letting me know, and tell me if there are updates. The ferries being down gutted her wedding plans, didn't they?"

"It's unfortunate, but we'll do our best to make her happy."

31

RHONDA, MAID OF HONOR

My friends and I piled into a restaurant by the ferry landing and grabbed a long table. While we waited on the Seattle side for hours, we drank cosmopolitans and skinny margaritas. I gulped down half a glass of water. I'd been drinking far too much before the wedding, and I didn't want to be plowed when we finally got to the island.

Pulling out my phone, I texted Claire for the tenth time since we'd been stuck here, left high and dry by a ferry's mechanical failure. The state ferry system had some old boats in the fleet, with gold bands around the smokestacks for fifty years in service, and our ferry was out of commission. We were told it'd be up and running sometime later today, maybe in three hours. But they'd already extended the deadline once because of a broken part.

My thumbs flew across my device, texting Claire. 'Sorry, I wish I was there. What a fiasco. We'll arrive as soon as we can. But it could be as late as eight tonight.'

A bridesmaid leaned over and said with boozy breath, "What's Claire saying?"

I pocketed my phone and shrugged. "It's really strange. I haven't heard from her in an hour. I hope she's all right. She must be having a meltdown."

Another bridesmaid winced. "Poor Claire. This is a nightmare of a wedding, with everything going wrong. It couldn't be going worse."

I said, "But I bet she'll wrestle it back into control. If anyone can do it, I know she will."

I motioned to the waitress and ordered another round for the table and assorted appetizers. Claire wasn't with us, but we might as well have fun while we waited.

32

CLAIRE'S FATHER

I sat in the car with Claire's grandmother on her mother's side. We'd just heard an update that the ferry delay would be longer than anticipated, and it'd be at least two more hours until the boat might be fixed.

I fiddled with my phone and texted Claire for the third time, saying, 'You were right. We should've gone to the island yesterday and stayed overnight. Not sure when we'll get there. Sending love, Dad.'

I sighed and turned to Hanna, my former wife's mother. She pursed her lips and stared straight ahead. She'd never liked me and today was pure torture for us to be packed in a car for hours waiting together.

Rain drops splatted against the windshield. I cleared my throat. "Tough luck about today. I bet you'd rather be home than stuck in a car with me on a rainy, windy day."

She sniffed. "You should be concerned with your daughter's ruined wedding right now, not my welfare. The poor girl. She must be weeping herself silly, and we're not there to comfort her."

I nodded. "You're right, as always. Have you heard from your daughter? I've been wondering where she is and how she's doing."

Hanna turned and scowled, pointing a finger at my face. "Listen up and listen good to me, young man."

I suppressed a smile, because I was in my mid-fifties. Trying to lighten the mood and inject a little humor, I said, "Thanks, I feel young at heart."

She studied me, narrowing her eyes, and I remembered why she'd always scared me deep down. Hanna was as frosty and cold as they come. But she was a tough bird, and I admired how she'd raised my former wife as a single mother. I knew being a single parent was a heavy load from taking care of Claire when she was young.

She said, "I'm not being funny. You have no business asking where she is, or how she's doing. After what you did to my daughter, you're the last person I'd tell. Even if the earth was burning up and we had seconds to live, I'd keep my trap shut. You blew it buster, when you took off with Claire in the camper bus and disappeared for years."

I cringed and squirmed in my seat. Blowing out a breath, I said, "Hanna, you are absolutely right, and I regret leaving your daughter at the campground and taking off. I shouldn't have taken Claire away from her mother. I was wrong, but at the time I thought it was for the best."

She crossed her arms. "You should've spoken with me before you did something that rash. I would've talked to Kendra and knocked some sense into her. She knew better than to drink during the day when she was taking care of Claire."

My throat tightened with tears. "I felt trapped and didn't know what to do. I had to get Claire away from Kendra's bad influence. It wasn't safe. It broke my heart, but she wouldn't stop drinking. She was drunk, Hanna, when she drove Claire to the playground while I worked a day job. She refused to get help."

She wiped tears from her cheeks. "I was sickened then by how she was spiraling down and defiant when I suggested she go to an AA meeting and speak to a counsellor. I was worried about all three of you back then. When you took off, I lost touch with Claire until she called and asked to live with me."

I nodded. "I can never thank you enough for taking her in and giving her a home."

Hanna reached over and patted my shoulder. "You're welcome. I'd do anything for that girl."

Rain drops splatted on the windshield, and I said, "Me too. Shall we take a walk? I have an umbrella in the car."

She chuckled and pulled up her raincoat hood. "Umbrellas are for sissies and people new to Seattle. I don't need one, but thanks for the offer. I'd like to get some fresh air. Let's walk to one of those restaurants."

We climbed out of the car and slammed the doors, making our way through the rain to a fish and chips shop. Clots of people stood under awnings outside. Inside, the restaurant was packed.

My stomach growled. "What can I get for you? I'll place an order at the window."

She smiled, and it was like the clouds parted. Her blue eyes beamed, and she looked twenty years younger. "I'd like a cup of black coffee and fish and chips with vinegar."

I grinned. "We'll make that two of the same. Wait here, I'll be right back."

I left her leaning under the awning and made my way to the end of the line at the order window outside. This could be the beginning of a new relationship with my former mother-in-law, and I was relieved to be starting over with her after a long period of antagonism between us. Our Grand Canyon of grief over Kendra's addiction broke us apart, but now we'd be on our way soon, I hoped, to my daughter's wedding.

I tapped a toe and waited as the line inched forward. Picking at a cuticle, I worried about my daughter's choice for her future husband. Ralph was known to tie one on with his friends, and I dearly hoped he wouldn't be a negative influence. Claire deserved only the best, especially today, despite rainy weather and ferry cancellations.

33

KENDRA, CLAIRE'S MOTHER

I stepped off a Barnacle Island bus and followed a sign pointing to The Farm. Trudging along, I shifted my backpack and wiped my brow. When Cousin Lacey tracked me down and emailed me, I was living in Spokane working at a women's shelter. I've worked hard to turn my life around but haven't been in contact with my family. I wanted to wait and prove to myself that this change was permanent before popping back into their lives as a new person.

Blisters throbbed on my aching feet. My hiking boots were worn, but I'd walked many a mile in them to get here. I stopped on a hill, looking down on The Farm, admiring the pastures around the structure where my daughter would be married today.

My pulse picked up, and I carried on. I wasn't sure how my surprise appearance would work out. Would

Claire scream at me? Would my own mother berate me for freezing her out for years? Would Claire's father accuse me of ruining our marriage by choosing alcohol over him and Claire?

Shifting my pack, I strode down the hill and hoped this afternoon and evening would turn into a joyous reunion. My daughter must be beautiful, and surrounded by her bridal party. My stomach fluttered with nerves, not knowing what I'd find.

I gnawed on my lower lip and walked down a gravel drive, wondering if I should wait to reintroduce myself to Claire, or get it over with right away. It might upset her if she spotted me before saying her vows, so I'd hide in the shadows, watch her get married and step out, giving her a hug before the reception.

Nodding to myself, I smiled, pleased with my plan. Everything was falling into place, and I was about to be reunited with my child.

34

CLAIRE

I stared at my cousin, my mind racing with ideas for how she might try to wreck my wedding. Thoughts flitted past, and I nodded to myself. Rain and ferry cancellations shredded my plans, and I was finished playing a nervous bride.

I gripped her shoulder and propelled her to the couch by the flickering warm fire. "Sit down and tell me what you did. Then I'll take a quick shower. Tell me everything now."

She swallowed and sat, perched on the edge of a gold velveteen sofa. Fiddling with her fingers, she said, "I'm not sure how to tell you this."

I sat next to her, drumming my fingers on the arm of the sofa. "I don't have time to play around. I have to get ready. Cough up the fur ball of whatever you did."

35

MACK, THE BEST MAN

Ralph and I stomped out of the cottage, slamming the door behind us. Ralph glanced at me and asked, "Where's your gear?"

"I'm leaving it here. I'll come back later to pick it up."

He clenched his jaw. "No, you're not. We'll be on our honeymoon, so no visitors allowed." He unlocked the door and swung it open, gesturing inside. "Get your stuff. I'll wait here. You're not coming back later."

I scowled. "Fine." I strode in, shoved my clothes, which were strewn on the floor, into my pack and lugged it out to the front porch. I sighed at my ruined plans to stay in the cottage at Ralph's expense. Now, what would I do?

Rain drummed down on the overhang over the front door, and Ralph said, "Just confirming, you'll drive my car after the wedding to Seattle and leave it at my place, correct?"

I nodded, looking forward to the trip. Living overseas and taking public transport for years meant I was rusty at driving, but I was sure it wouldn't pose a problem. "Right-o, consider it done, my man."

I tossed my pack in his backseat and climbed in the passenger seat. Driving slowly away, he pointed to the ten mile an hour speed limit sign on the dirt road. "People in this hollow are crazy, but Claire and I love it here."

He scratched his wrist, and I reached over, swatting his hand. "Stop that. You don't want to have red welts when you're standing at the altar."

Silence fell in the car. I checked my man-bun and turned to him. "Hey, man, where am I going to stay tonight?"

He shrugged. "Claire might've made arrangements. We'll ask her. She said something about camping in yurts, if I heard right, for guests who stayed overnight."

I looked out the side window and rolled my eyes. I hadn't come all the way from Asia for his wedding to camp out and hurt my back. Besides, where was I going to host my podcast tomorrow? I'd have to look into using a room at The Farm for free. Maybe they'd put me up for a few nights for free or charge it to Ralph's credit card, and I could use one of their meeting rooms.

"Sounds good," I said, clapping him on the shoulder. "Big day for you. How're you feeling?"

I sang a few bars of a song about going to the chapel of love, and he winced. "Stop, stop. I'll do whatever you say, just don't sing."

I sat back and smiled. Being the youngest in my family, I felt my best when I was truly getting on someone's nerves.

He said, "I'm super nervous, more than I've ever been. My skin is itching. I'm hungover with a raging headache. But I'm ready."

"Glad to hear it."

He drove along a winding road past pastures, barns and old houses. On a straightaway, he glanced over. "You have the rings, don't you?"

I patted my empty pockets, and a cold chill crept up my spine. "Uh, buddy, I don't know how to say this, but I don't have them."

He tipped his head back and laughed. Pounding a fist on the steering wheel, he said, "I thought you might forget, so I took them with me. I'll give them to you right before the ceremony."

I sheepishly said, "Good call, man. We've got it covered."

36

MEG

Troy and I worked seamlessly in the kitchen, gliding around each other and avoiding collisions. I assigned Francesca the task of checking on the cake to make sure it wasn't sliding and helping Troy, who was a whiz with a knife.

Troy hollered over his shoulder to me, "Franny's set to plate the salads and serve soup and salads, when it's time."

Wiping my hands on my apron, I said, "Sounds like we're ready."

I rested a hand on my churning stomach, because although we had the meal prepped as much as we could, I had a dark feeling of foreboding. Something about this wedding wasn't right.

I shuddered and blew out a breath. "I'll be glad when

this one's in the books, and we're on to the next one tomorrow."

Troy came over to me and said in a low voice, "Having French dip sandwiches is kind of odd to eat at a wedding, isn't it?"

Francesca put a hand on her hip and smiled. "I like their unconventional menu. It takes courage to veer from the norm."

I shot a last look at the kitchen, checking saucepans and the tall pot with butternut squash soup. "Looks like we're as set as we can be. Let's change aprons and freshen up."

Francesca grinned and pushed her younger brother aside. "I'm first. I call the bathroom."

She hurried away, and I turned to Troy. We smiled at each other and rolled our eyes. I was lucky to have two beautiful grown children who lived near me on Barnacle Island. When my former husband left us one Christmas Eve years ago, we were emotional shipwrecks. In some ways, we're still damaged from his cruel act and clinging to the wreckage, but with our love, our smaller family was intact.

I shrugged. Along with the bitter came the sweet. Francesca, Troy and I were a stew of ingredients, blending together and stronger for having been abandoned by their father.

I wiped tears from my eyes, wishing the bride the best,

But deep in my heart, I wished I was young again and starting over, with my whole life ahead of me. Oh, to be young and beautiful, glowing with joy.

RALPH, THE GROOM

Mack gave me the silent treatment on the way to The Farm. He probably expected me to shell out for a fancy place for him to stay tonight or for a week or more, but I was done being the one who paid for everything.

I shook my head. Although he was best man, he avoided paying the bar tab last night. He hurried to the bathroom and hid in there until I paid with my credit card, which I don't like to do.

Bitter bile crept up the back of my throat, and I told myself to shrug off my irritation at Mack about money and ignore my itching skin from poison oak exposure. Combined with a whopping hangover, all these factors threatened to ruin the rest of the day I'd long anticipated.

I hummed to myself to improve my mood, because

nothing was going to ruin my wedding day. I'd looked forward to this ever since I laid eyes on Claire, which was a month before I broke things off with Belle.

I swallowed hard. I had to keep that fact from both Belle and Claire, because neither one suspected I was a double-timing creep. I didn't want anyone to find out I'd been unfair to Belle. At the wedding, I'd make sure the two women didn't meet and compare notes to keep my secret safe.

Rubbing my right temple, I moaned. I should never have caved to Belle's pressure and invited her to the wedding. I needed a better backbone, if I hoped to survive my marriage.

Mack reached over, tapping my arm. "Everything okay, buddy? I'm here for you. Don't worry."

I nodded, but doubted he could step in and do the job of best man with ease. He was more of a self-centered everything is about me kind of guy who loved to go out and have a good time on someone else's dime. I never should have succumbed to his wheedling over the phone and by texts and emails and invited him to be my best man.

Bile crept up my throat, and I coughed, wincing at the price of the plane ticket I bought for him to attend the biggest day of my life. We'd been friends since preschool, and at the time, I was glad to pay for his flights.

I sighed and turned left down a road leading to The

Farm, passing a woman wearing worn hiking boots and a backpack. She strode with meaning and purpose down the lane, and I hoped she wasn't heading to my wedding. Someone looking like that didn't belong at our event.

38

COUSIN LACEY

I drew a deep breath and decided to not tell the complete truth to Claire. My cousin didn't need to know the full extent of my plans to ruin her happiness today. She was being kind, even though I barely knew her, but it was time to confess part of what I'd done.

Regret twisted in my gut. I'd made a mistake, but it was too late to stop the train from rolling. I stood and paced, stopping in front of the fireplace. "I'm sorry, but I believe the bouquet might contain a certain flower you're allergic to."

Her mouth fell open. "What?"

I shrugged. "But at least you know now, ahead of time."

She narrowed her eyes. "What did you put in there?"

I tilted my head. "I called your florist and said you

wanted them to add a lily, you know the ones that made you sneeze when you and your dad visited?"

Her hands clenched. "I'll take it out. Is there anything else?"

My shoulders rose to my ears. "I'm really sorry about this, but I was going to slip poison hemlock into your bouquet at the last minute. But I left it outside, so no one's in danger. Just breathing the pollen could harm your lungs and make you sick."

She shook her head. "You're sick in the head to think of these things. You resorted to crazy extremes, just because I didn't pick you to be in the bridal party?"

I slumped into a chair, my face heating and burning with shame. I wished I could disappear and melt into the rug. "I'm sorry is all I can say. I was angry and couldn't help myself. But you're right. I need help."

She stood and bit her lip. "Thank you for telling me. Let's put it behind us for the moment and get ready. I'll shower, and you can help me get dressed. We don't have much time."

I nodded. "Okay. You're being so nice about this. I can't believe it."

While she took a shower, I paced in front of the fire, wishing I could cancel the other bad things coming her way. But it was too late. The actors were already on their way from Oak Harbor, and they weren't answering my texts.

39

BELLE

Heading south on Highway 20, I followed signs to The Farm and drove past the town of Greenbank, which was a few old buildings, houses and barns. On my left, I could see Baby Head Island and a long bay with gray, choppy water. A gust of wind buffeted my car as I sped along.

Whistling a dreary dirge, I nodded to a sign advertising The Farm and turned left down a private lane. I felt the potential for violence roiling in my veins. Ralph needed to be taught a lesson, and I'd take Claire down with him at the same time. I'll figure out exactly what to do when I get there and assess the situation.

Maybe I'll grab the microphone and announce what he did to me and humiliate him. Maybe I'll choke him with his tie. I'll survey the grounds for potential weapons and death traps before going inside.

I pulled up and parked at the end of the parking lot and slid out of my car, quietly closing the door, so as not to attract attention. Rain pattered down on my head, and I put up an umbrella, taking a look around.

An old cistern stood in the back of the property, and I made my way down a gravel drive to examine it closer. A steady breeze pushed strands of hair in my face, and I pulled them away to see better.

Rain drops fell on the umbrella, and my feet were getting wet standing on cold, damp ground. Gazing at a ladder going up the side of the massive cistern, I nodded. That would do for my purposes, and I'd end my showdown there. They'd never see it coming on their happy day.

40

FRANCESCA

Gazing out a kitchen window, I paused my dishwashing and turned off the water. A suspicious-looking woman walked down the drive, looking around as if checking to see if someone was watching her. She held a big black umbrella over her head and stopped to stare at an old cistern out back. She went over to a ladder on it and tugged, before stepping back and smiling.

Troy marched inside, his short sandy brown hair dripping wet from taking trash outside to a dumpster out back. He said to me, "What're you doing?"

In a low voice, I said, "Watching that woman. She strikes me as odd, like she's up to no good."

Troy rapped on the window, and the women jumped in the air. She pointed a finger at us and frowned, marching away to the front of the building.

My brother and I chuckled, and I said, "I hope she doesn't report us for bothering her. I don't want to get in trouble. I need this job."

He bumped my shoulder. "I know what you mean. Bills have to be paid. Baby needs bread, and the dough must roll in."

We laughed, but when I snorted, Mom called, "What're you two doing over there? Get back to work."

We snickered behind our hands and returned to our tasks. I shook my head at how I couldn't wait for this day to end. My feet throbbed. My fingers were wrinkled from washing dishes. My back ached. And the wedding and dinner hadn't even begun.

41

CLAIRE

Going into the bathroom, I locked the door, in case my angry weird cousin tried to pull a trick while I was vulnerable. I stepped out of my jeans and shirt and pulled a shower cap over my hair to keep it dry. Turning on the water on in a large tiled shower, I sighed as hot water pounded on my back.

Scrubbing, I let my anxiety flow with the water down the drain. Worrying hadn't helped, so I'd go with the flow and be a relaxed bride from now on. The worst had happened, with the ferry boats down and Lacey plotting to poison me with a toxic flower. Nothing else would go wrong, and if it did, I'd laugh it off and deal with it.

I smiled and turned off the water, drying with a white fluffy oversized bath towel. Reminded of the cottage on the island where we'd spend our honeymoon, I sighed, wishing Ralph hadn't insisted on staying there. I'd wanted to go to Bali or Fiji or Paris, but no, he put his foot down and insisted the cottage was perfect, because it cost far less than what I wanted, and we had fond memories from staying there in the past.

I shook my head, wishing locals in the hollow weren't as nosy and combative, seeing every strange car and new person as a threat to their precious private road.

Leaving the bathroom, I stepped into the room and gasped.

My cousin Lacey stood in front of a blazing fire. She smiled and gestured to my white lace wedding dress, laid over the back of the sofa. My white shoes waited for me to slip into them.

She gestured to the veil and said, "Let's get you dressed."

A tear slid down my cheek, and I swallowed, releasing the dream I'd held onto for years of a wedding with friends and a honeymoon on a tropical island or in Europe. I missed Rhonda and my father and grandma, but this was the reality before me.

I smiled, wiped away a tear. "Thanks. I appreciate it. The show will go on."

As I stepped into the dress, I couldn't help but check the fabric for tears and rips. As long as I lived, I'd bear a grudge against Lacey and be suspicious of her. But these were my last moments of being single, and I shouldn't dwell on her betrayal.

She zipped up the back of the dress. I brushed my hair

and added makeup. I stepped into the shoes, and she helped me put on my white wedding veil with a long train. Standing in front of a gold-framed mirror, I grinned.

"I look like a bride, don't I?"

Lacey nodded. "You're beautiful, and your dress is perfect."

"Thanks. Now let's go out there and get this over with."

She opened the door, and I glided through, inwardly bidding my single days goodbye. I paused, and she gathered my train.

"Got it?" I said.

"Sure, do. Lacey at your service."

"Come on, maid of honor, we've got a rodeo to attend."

But as I stepped ahead toward my new future, a feeling of foreboding swept over me, and I shuddered and stopped in the hall.

Lacey said, "Everything okay?"

"Yeah, I think so. I just had the oddest feeling though." I shivered and straightened up, with my shoulders back. "Okay, this is it, my big moment, Onward we go."

42

KENDRA

Hearing footsteps coming down the hall, I stepped into a dark alcove to hide. My pulse picked up, and my hands turned cold. I couldn't let my daughter discover I was here, not yet. I wanted to wait until after the ceremony, so I wouldn't distract from her special moment. No one wants a mother of the bride at a wedding to turn the attention on herself, which is what I'd do if I introduced myself to her too soon.

Claire swept past me, walking tall with her shoulders back, just like I taught her to when she was young. Tears streamed down my cheeks, and I let out a little burble of grief for all I'd missed. She was a woman now, not the child who was taken from me unfairly.

Another young woman was with Claire, and she passed by, holding the train. She locked eyes with me and shook her head before continuing on.

I clapped a hand over my mouth and pivoted around, facing a dark door. Closing my eyes, I heard Claire say, 'What was that? Did you hear a strange sound just now?"

Lacey said, "Probably just the wind is all. Nothing to worry about."

43

COUSIN LACEY

Following Claire down the hall, we passed someone lurking in a dark doorway. My eyes just about popped out when I saw an older woman resembling Claire.

Carrying the train above the carpet, I shook my head vigorously at Kendra to communicate she should leave. Our plan was kaput. She needed to go. I changed my mind and didn't want to be party to her kersplat all over the wedding. My cousin Claire was too nice to smash it to smithereens.

I tried to hiss something to Kendra, but she whipped around, turning to face a door. The moment passed, and it was too late to get a message to the woman who could wreck Claire's idyllic wedding. I'll look for Kendra later and tell her to disappear before she breaks Claire's heart again.

Claire said, "Did you hear a strange noise just now?"

"Probably just the wind. It's really starting to blow outside. Hey, can I ask you a question?"

"Sure, what is it?"

"What would you do if your mother showed up today at your wedding?"

Claire stopped suddenly, and I bumped into her. She whipped around and said, "Never mention her to me again, especially not today. If she showed up at my wedding, I'd have her hauled away for barging into a private party. She left me. There's no curing a heartache like that."

I nodded and kept my trap shut about the truth. Apparently her dad didn't tell her he took Claire. Her mom didn't leave her. It was the other way around.

Claire sniffed and wiped her nose with the back of her hand. "Do you have a tissue?"

I pulled a fresh one out of my pocket, handing it to her. "At your service and sorry I asked."

She dabbed her eyes, blew her nose and took a deep breath. We marched ahead to her event, which I envied more than anything in my life. In my small town, there wasn't a glimmer of hope for my being a bride.

A heavy feeling of regret mixed with dread soured my stomach. Maybe the actors I hired wouldn't show up. That would be for the best.

44

FRANCESCA

I sidled up to Mom and said in a low voice, "Is it okay if I go watch the wedding?"

Mom set down a stirring spoon. "No, it's not okay, sweetheart. I need you in the kitchen working."

I gestured to the empty sink. "But there's nothing to do until I serve the soup and salad courses."

Mom said, "We're not guests, and we shouldn't stand on the sidelines for that poor bride's wedding. She's had enough go wrong as it is today."

I nodded. "Okay, understood."

Troy swept by, nudging me with his elbow. "Hey, get to work, lazy bones. What're you doing standing there? Hup to, let's go."

Mom grinned, and I smiled. All was right with our world, for a brief moment at least.

45

CLAIRE

Rain drummed down on the roof, and my heart fluttered at the sight of Ralph wearing a black tuxedo standing by the fireplace. Music at my wedding was out, because the musicians I'd hired were from Seattle, and they were stuck on the other side of Puget Sound, along with the DJ with dance music, who was waiting for the same ferry boat.

Lacey whispered, "Ready?"

I gulped. "As much as I'll ever be."

Someone moved on the periphery, and I glanced over to see who it was, but no one was there. Maybe I was nervous enough that I was imagining things. I shrugged and made my way to Ralph and his goofy best friend Mack.

Ralph stood tall, grinning at me, and Mack slouched

with a hand in his pocket. But as soon as Mack saw Lacey, his eyes lit up, and he beamed.

Images I'd imagined over the years for this moment flitted through my mind, and I smiled. None of my little girl's dreams added up to this strange surreal wedding with no guests. But the funny thing was, it didn't matter. I'd blown out of proportion the stuff that event planners cared about, but my heart was all that mattered.

A mirror reflected bright light, and I blinked, turning away. White spots swam before my eyes. I stumbled, righting myself.

A woman who looked slightly familiar stood in the shadows, glaring. She bore a strong resemblance to Ralph's former girlfriend, but Belle couldn't be here. It was crazy of me to imagine I saw her at my wedding.

Holding on to the back of a chair, I looked around and caught a quick glimpse of an older woman who looked a bit like my mother. I touched my forehead, feeling woozy. Was I having hallucinations?

I hadn't seen or spoken with my mother since she abandoned me. I specifically told Dad and Grandma I'd disown them if they tracked her down to say I was getting married. Mom could not be and should not be here.

Swallowing hard, I took small steps toward Ralph and stood on wobbly legs near the fireplace. A trickle of cold sweat ran down the insides of my arms, and I clamped my arms tight to my chest. Looking down at the flowers in my hands, I spotted the lily I'd failed to remove and sneezed.

Lacey reached around and plucked the offending flower from the bridal bouquet. She whispered, "Sorry," and set it down by the window.

Candy, the event manager, smiled. "Are you ready? Shall we go ahead?"

A headache throbbed, and a band of cold pain wrapped tight around my head. I winced. Not now, I told my body. This is not a time for a blinding migraine. You can come back in a week or ten, but just go away. Let me get through this one day.

Ralph whispered, "You look beautiful. Everything okay?"

I touched my head. "I feel a migraine coming on."

Turning to Candy, the event manager, who would officiate our wedding, since Dad was stuck on the Seattle side, I said, "Could I please have two extra-strength pain relievers, a Diet Coke and a cup of black coffee?"

Candy nodded. "Of course, I'll be right back with that."

Ralph said, "Hon, I'm sorry you're not feeling well. Do you think we should postpone the ceremony?"

I rested a hand on the fireplace mantel and sighed. "I'm not sure. Let me think about it. I hope the caffeine will help."

Out of the corner of my eyes, I saw Mack wiggle his fingers and smile at Lacey, and she grinned, showing a gap between her two front teeth. I half-smiled, thinking they could be sweet together.

I said to Ralph, "Would you please move that lily outside? It might be contributing to my headache."

Mack said, "I'll move it for you. The best man helps whenever he can. Ask me, and I'm your man."

He strode over to the flower, and Lacey hustled after him. Together, they lifted the offending lily, where a huge yellow stamen fairly dripped with potent pollen that irritated my sinuses. Opening the door, they threw it out into the rain and gently closed the door, whispering to each other.

"Sit down," Ralph said, helping me into a chair.

I plopped down, set my bouquet on my lap and massaged my temples.

A kitchen helper in a green apron approached me. She carried a serving tray with a soda pop, a cup of coffee and two white pain reliever tablets.

With a sudden jarring sound, the door burst open. Two men in firefighter gear strode inside, grinning from ear to ear. Singing a bawdy song, they stripped down to their boxer shorts, tossing clothes around the room. Their naked abdomens rippled with muscles.

My headache throbbed. The kitchen helper tripped and fell toward me. Coffee and pop flew into the air, covering me. I shrieked, raising my hands, but hot coffee burned my chest and stained my white lace wedding dress. Pills flew in the air.

My mouth dropped open, and I wondered who had the audacity to order strippers on my wedding day.

The kitchen helper's cheeks blazed bright red, and she picked up the empty coffee cup and pop can, fleeing with her tray to the kitchen.

I glanced at Ralph, and slight smiles grew on our faces until we burst out laughing. This was ludicrous. At least we were alive and no one died on my wedding day.

We all guffawed and chuckled, including the male strippers who were gathering their gear. I was out of breath from laughing so hard, and tense muscles in my back relaxed.

I stood in my sopping wet, muddy brown dress and said, "This is the weirdest wedding I've ever been to."

Ralph said, "Me too."

The strippers quickly dressed and waved, slipping out the door.

"Count me in on that," Mack said.

Looking around the room, I noticed the white spots in my field of vision were less visible. I said, "Does anyone know who sent the strippers?"

A small voice spoke up. Cousin Lacey stared at the floor and said, "I did it, and I'll be eternally sorry. When you were so nice to me, Claire, in the bridal suite, it was too late to cancel. I couldn't get a hold of the strippers in time to stop them."

Mack chuckled, covering his mouth. Ralph laughed. I couldn't help but smile and shrug.

The kitchen helper rushed in the room and bent

down, mopping up the spilled mess with rags and paper towels.

Looking down at my ruined dress, I said to her, "Would you please go in the kitchen and get me more of what you brought the first time? Thanks very much."

Candy appeared, wringing her hands and frowning. "Oh, Claire, I'm so sorry about this. We'll pay to get it drycleaned and see if we can get out the stain. In the meantime, I'll get what you asked for and bring it myself."

I whooshed out a breath and sat, relaxing in warmth from the fire. Candy appeared and handed me a can of pop and two pain relievers, which I quickly swallowed. I gulped the liquid and hoped the caffeine would magically make my early migraine symptoms dissipate. But then Ralph said something that set my teeth on edge.

46

RALPH

I handed Claire two tablets and watched her gulp them down, chugging the pop. I stopped myself from rolling my eyes because really, how bad was a migraine? I didn't think it was a big deal, at least not how she made it out to be. But I put up with her antics. When she said she saw spots and had blinding headaches, I knew it was merely a call for attention. I cut her slack because of the strange way she was brought up by her father, living on the road, and later with her grandmother.

Clearing my throat, I picked up Claire's cup of coffee and drank most of it. Setting the cup down beside Claire for her to finish, she cocked her head and gave me a slight glare, which wasn't right on our wedding day. We were about to get hitched forever, so she shouldn't flash me a scolding look.

I frowned at her in return, just to get even. Whatever was bugging her must be some little thing only she knew about. She picked up the cup and sipped coffee, leaning back in the chair and letting out a sigh.

I turned to Mack and Lacey, who was crazy for hiring strippers to invade our wedding. I'd talk to Claire later about how I really felt about it, but now was not the time. I'd laugh now but blame her later for letting a wackdoodle cousin destroy our wedding ceremony.

Candy, the officiant and events manager, said, "I'll go check on something and be right back to check if you're ready to get started."

"Thank you," Claire said, in a voice that sounded hard with a less eager tone to get married than say, last week, or yesterday. Were we getting on each other's nerves? Were we making a mistake? Was her headache a sign we shouldn't marry? I certainly had doubts racing through my mind like a raging forest fire. I mean, when she asked for pop and coffee, she should've asked me if I wanted some. That's part of being in a partnership.

I clapped my hands. "Hey, I wanted to say something. I planned to say it during dinner, but why wait?"

Claire winced when I clapped. Mack nodded. Lacey played with a strand of her long red hair.

"I've started a honeymoon crowdfunding page for us, so if you'd like to contribute and help us out, please donate, the more the better!"

Claire pressed her lips together in a tight, flat line and stared at the fire. Her eye twitched, and her jaw clenched.

I clapped her on the shoulder, and she spilled the rest of her coffee on her dress. "Isn't that right, Claire Bear? We'd really appreciate the help."

She said, "I wish you'd told me about this before. It's the first I've heard of it."

Candy entered the room and came over to us. "I'm sorry to interrupt, but would you like to get started?"

Claire stood, and I smiled at her, but she wouldn't meet my gaze. I had no idea what was ticking her off. I was only trying to take advantage of the giving opportunity, so the wedding didn't put us deeper in debt.

She pointed at me and said in a stern voice, "I think it would be much better if we ate dinner before we were married. That way, it gives a few stragglers time to drive around and see the ceremony. Does that make sense to you?"

I opened my hands and shrugged. "Sure, it sounds good. Whatever you say. Will that work for your schedule, Candy?"

She nodded. "Whatever you'd like. I'll let the kitchen know you're ready to sit and eat dinner."

Claire and I said at the same time, "Thank you."

But somehow my future wife's tone of voice sounded suddenly harsh, as if something had changed within her in the last hour, and she was an octave below and less optimistic than when she drove over and spoke with me at the cottage. I had no idea what changed. Oh well, it'd be one of those mysteries between us, and I didn't need to worry about it.

47

FRANCESCA

I rushed back into the kitchen, set the tray down and blew out a breath. Mom said, "What happened out there and why's the coffee cup empty already?"

Cringing, I coughed up the truth. "Male strippers came in when I was serving the coffee and pop. I got distracted and tripped."

Mom clapped a hand to her mouth. "Oh, honey, that's not good. We need to keep in their good graces, so they'll recommend us and give us a good rating and tell other people to hire us to cater their event."

I grabbed a bunch of rags and paper towels. "I've got to clean up what I spilled."

Mom said in a whisper, "What did you spill and where?"

I swallowed, and my mouth was dry. I winced. "I

spilled coffee and pop on the floor and on the bride's dress."

Mom's mouth dropped opened wide, and I could see her back molars. "Oh, sweetie, run to clean it up."

I rushed out, mopped up the floor and hurried back to the kitchen, dumping the paper towels in the trash and the rags in the laundry bin. I said to Mom, "I don't think I'm cut out for this line of work."

She waved a hand. "Nonsense, you just need to get your sea legs. I'm sure you'll be fine when it comes to serving the soup course."

I nodded, wanting to please her. "I'll try my best. Thanks for the vote of confidence."

Troy said, "You can do it, Franny. You'll be great."

I grinned at him, but secretly doubted he and Mom were right. But at least no matter what, I knew my family would have my back.

48

MEG

My throat tightened with tears, and I blinked hard. If Francesca didn't vastly improve her serving skills, I'd have to fire my daughter when the night was over. But she needed the money, and I wanted to keep her on.

When Francesca grabbed rags and paper towels, rushing out of the kitchen, Troy patted my shoulder. "You're doing a good job, Mom. She'll come around. We just need to be patient with her."

I blew out a breath. "I hope so. I really don't want to have to let her go."

Candy strode in the kitchen and came over. In a low urgent voice, she said, "We have a change in plan. The wedding ceremony is postponed until after dinner, due to your daughter's disaster just now."

I bit my lip. "I'm so sorry. I'll pay for cleaning the wedding dress."

Candy shook her head. "We'll cover it as part of our business expenses. But we can't have it happen again."

I shook my head. "Definitely not. I'll make sure of it. You can count on me."

She nodded. "Okay, let's move on. They want to eat right away, and there's only four of them."

Francesca breezed into the kitchen, her cheeks rosy red. "But I saw two women hanging around. Are they with the wedding party?"

We all shrugged. Candy said, "Let's get to it. Soup course is on. Everyone, hop to."

I nodded to my kids. "You heard what she said. We'll serve the butternut squash soup, salads after that, then sandwiches."

49

MACK

When Ralph brought up the topic of money, I figured it was my opening to mention I was broke and needed a handout. I smiled at him and went over, clapping him on the back. "Hey, since you mentioned money, I need to ask if you can lend me five thou. I'm stuck stateside and need to get back to my place."

His eyes opened wide. "What're you talking about? I bought you a round-trip ticket for the wedding."

Claire tugged on Ralph's hand. "Wait, you said you wouldn't pay for his trip, and we had to limit our wedding budget. Why did you pay for his plane ticket, but I had to cut fifty guests from the list?"

Ralph's Adam's apple bobbed up and down. He ran a finger around his shirt collar and loosened his tie. "Things had to be done to get Mack here to be my best man."

Claire frowned. "You could've gotten someone who lived in the same country or even the same state, since you like to save money so much."

I tilted my head and tried to tamp down the negative energy. "Hey, let's not argue. Sorry I brought up the subject."

Claire and Ralph frowned, but Lacey sidled over, slipping her warm hand into mine. I smiled at her and said to Ralph, "Seriously, man, I need to get back to Thailand. I've got business there to attend to and a podcast to run."

Ralph's face flushed. "Sorry, but you're on your own. Let's go eat dinner. I'm starved."

Claire took off her veil and train, leaving them on a chair.

As we walked to the dining room, I noticed Claire and Ralph were not arm in arm. I got the feeling they were miles apart regarding their views on money, which wasn't good in my humble opinion.

Lacey leaned in. "What do you need to run a podcast?"

"Good gear, which I brought with me. And strong internet service."

She smiled. "Not to be too bold, but where I live, we've got good internet service and nice people. You could move in with me and run your podcast there."

I let go of her hand. "But we just met. I couldn't take advantage of you like that. It wouldn't be fair."

She smiled. "Let's see how the evening goes. We could

try it out on a trial basis for a few weeks. We might find we're better suited for each other than these two."

I tipped back my head and laughed, and she joined in. I liked how she let a loud laugh rip and snorted, as if she didn't care what anyone else thought about her. Wrapping my arms around her and drawing her close, I said, "You might be my kind of girl. Let's talk at the end of the evening."

50

COUSIN LACEY

When the male strippers barged in the room, I thought I'd shrivel up and die right then and there. But I was lucky when Claire laughed, and we all joined in. Thank goodness, finally, for a little levity in this uptight group.

The guy with the man bun, Mr. Best Man, shot me smiles, which I hadn't experienced since high school. It'd been such a long drought, my heart skipped a beat, My pulse picked up, and my stomach got the wigglies. I felt funny inside, just looking at him.

Claire and Ralph weren't getting along so well, from my point of view. I was surprised they were talking about going ahead with the ceremony after dinner, because fractious agitation was the dominant emotion I'd observed between them. I'd run like hell from him if I were her. I mean, who turns their wedding into a fundraiser? That's just crass.

I slipped my hand into Mack's, and as we walked into dinner together, I decided to take the plunge and possibly import a potential partner to my small town. It couldn't hurt to try, so why not invite him to share my living space. What I didn't tell him was that I lived in a small trailer that was hot in summer, but he didn't need to find that out until he moved in.

51

BELLE

When the four dinner guests were seated in the dining room, I crept around the corner, peering in and watching for the right time to make my grand entrance. I'd take Ralph down a notch, and Claire too, while I was at it. They deserved to hurt, given how horrible he was to me. The truth will come out about how I bet he two-timed me.

But just as I was about to step into the dining room, another woman looked in and caught my attention. She was dressed in hiking boots, a blue sweatshirt and faded jeans. Her cheeks were ruddy, like she'd been out in the wind, and she didn't look like she was with the catering company. She glared at me and shook her head, pointing to the dining room and wagging a finger.

My pulse quickened, because I wouldn't let a stranger in hiking boots tell me what to do. I frowned at her. The older woman wanted to squash my moment, but I'd go ahead anyway. As I took a step into the dining room, the best man stood up, raising a glass of red wine.

He said, "I'd like to make a toast to the best guy around. There couldn't be a finer man to marry Claire, who he says is his best friend. Let's drink to their happiness."

They raised their glasses and took a sip. Mack stomped a foot on the floor, and floorboards vibrated under my feet. He repeated the gesture and said, "Let's give it up for the groom. Come on, man, give a toast."

Ralph smiled, smoothing his black tuxedo. I grimaced, because that's what we agreed he'd wear on our wedding day, which was supposed to be today. I gritted my teeth and seethed. I'd listen to his stupid toast and then obliterate their oblivious, idiotic happiness. I'd bring them down and meddle with their mindsets, so they'll beg for mercy and hate each other on the spot.

A server wearing a green apron came out of the kitchen carrying two bowls of what looked like butternut squash soup. Her curly dark hair was pulled back in a ponytail, and her cheeks where rosy red.

Just as she approached, Ralph suddenly stood up, and two bowls of soup spilled and splashed all over his tuxedo, drenching him. He spluttered and wiped soup from his face with his hands.

Mack laughed and stomped a foot on the floor, clapping his hands. A redhead near him tipped back her head and snorted, letting out raucous laughter.

Claire jumped up and pointed at the cake. "Stop, Mack. The cake is moving."

He chuckled and waved a hand. Ralph wiped his face with a hideous yellow napkin. The top part of the cake slowly tipped over and fell with a soft splat on the sheet cake below.

A collective groan went up from the group. I put a hand over my mouth, hiding a smile. This was bad, very bad indeed.

Tears streamed down the server's face as she apologized over and over. She collected broken bowls from the floor and rushed into the kitchen.

Ralph shook a fist at the server's back. "I'll have you fired for that. I rented this tux, and I have to return it in pristine condition."

Claire sighed, studying the mess of a wedding cake, and went over to Ralph. Holding out her hands, she said, "Calm down, she didn't mean to do it. It's your fault anyway. You stood up when she was serving you."

He turned on her, glaring, his eyes narrow slits. I'd seen that look before, and it was ugly. He said, "No one tells me to calm down. Get away from me and fix your damned cake. That's all you cared about anyway."

I cocked my head. At this rate, they didn't need much help from me to create frisson and fracture their joy. As far as I saw, all joy had left the room a long time ago.

She crossed her arms. "Fine, have it your way and sit in a damp suit for all I care. And that cake is not all I care about. I care about us and our future."

He paused a beat and nodded. "I'm sorry, I shouldn't have said those mean things."

"I accept your apology, and I'm not perfect either."

I nodded to myself. This was my cue to step in and push them apart. The hiker woman started to walk in the room, striding with meaning and purpose. But I wasn't going to let anyone steal my thunder. This was my time to shine and break the man who crippled me emotionally.

Going up to Ralph, I poked a finger in his face. "You weasel, I bet you two-timed me with her before dumping me."

A look of fear flickered in his eyes, and he blinked, the way he did when he was wrong, and I'd caught him in a lie. His Adam's apple bobbed up and down. "I don't know what you're talking about."

I marched over to the cake, shoved my hand down deep into thick gooey frosting and sponge cake. Grabbing a fistful, I aimed, throwing it at Ralph's face.

The room went still and silent. Frosting clung to his cheeks, eyes and black tuxedo. It looked like a confetti bomb exploded.

I said in my most threatening, commanding voice that made my staff wither at work, motivated by fear of being fired, "You're the worst liar in the world. It's clear you cheated on me from your reaction. You're a horrible person."

He grunted and wiped cake from his eyes, throwing it down in a puddle of creamy orange soup on the floor. He pointed to the door. "Get out Belle. You'd better leave right now."

Claire slapped her hands against the sides of her muddy brown stained white lace wedding dress. "Who is this? Ralph, do you know her?"

The kitchen server emerged from the kitchen just then, carrying two hot steaming bowls of soup in her hands.

I rushed over to Claire, grabbed her arm and twisted it around her back. We bumped into the server, soup sloshed over the sides and the bowls fell with a clatter to the floor.

The server clapped a hand to her mouth and fled to the kitchen, leaving the wreckage behind.

I hissed into Claire's ear. "You're coming with me. We're going on a little side trip, you cheater. This won't take long."

52

CLAIRE

I wriggled and fought with my fists, trying to extricate myself from the stranger's tight grip. But she had a firm hold on me and wouldn't let go.

I threw myself into Ralph. "Help me. Get her away from me."

But he stepped back and held up his hands, as if surrendering. Whoever this woman was, she held some sort of power over him. Or was he just a coward who wouldn't stand up for me? It was ridiculous that this close to getting married, I was finally seeing what he was made of and that he had no backbone or urge to defend me. This wasn't a man I wanted to marry.

Yanking away from her firm grip, I slipped in frosting, cake and spilled squash soup, falling down in the mess Ralph created. I scrambled to find firm footing and jumped to my feet, barking at Belle, who must be a former girlfriend of his, "Leave me alone."

She advanced on me, and I grabbed a long knife from the cake table, holding it out in front of me. I'd had the silver-plated knife engraved with our names. Well, that turned out to be a total waste. I saw clearly how I'd frittered away my time and energy with him. Our bickering about money signaled how vastly different the small man in a ruined black tux was from me, but I'd ignored the waving red flags.

Belle moved closer, her hands out in a fighter's stance.

My hands trembled, holding the knife. My pulse raced.

Ralph waved his hands slowly in the air, as if this was a joke, and said in a sing-song voice, "Come on, girls, cut it out. Don't fight over me."

My mouth fell open. How self-centered was he? Didn't he see this woman, who was apparently a former girlfriend, was out to hurt me?

Belle ripped the knife out of my hands. She grabbed my wrist, flipped me around and held my wrists in her muscled hands. She said in a stern voice, "Come with me. We're going outside, where you'll learn there are consequences for heart breakers like you who break up long-term relationships."

I pulled away and tugged at my wrists, kicking at her knees and shins, but couldn't get away from her. I bet Belle worked out regularly, because her muscles even in her fingers were much stronger than mine. I said, "I don't know who you are."

She tightened her grip. "You took him from me."

My face heated, and I gasped. "He said he was single when we met."

"You lie, just like he does. Come with me. I have a special treat waiting for you on your wedding day."

She hustled me toward the French doors leading outside, where rain pelted down. I struggled and squealed.

Candy, the events manager, came in the room and stopped short, staring at the mutilated wedding cake and the knife in Belle's hand. She said, "I'll call the police."

Belle said to Ralph, "This is your chance to save your beloved bride, if you had any guts."

He held up his hands. "No, you're a crazy woman. I'll let the police handle it when they get here to deal with you. You're a psycho."

Belle spat on the floor. "You said you loved me, and you proposed to me. We were supposed to be married on this very day." She yanked my wrists behind my back. "Did you know that, Claire, when you went after another woman's man?"

I lied to protect myself. "I didn't know. I had no idea."

Belle marched me to the door, but I resisted with every muscle in my body. I screamed, "I could use some help. Lacey? Mack?"

I craned my head, but they were gone. Apparently,

they disappeared when the fighting started. Belle was about to propel me outside when an older woman in hiking boots and jeans and a sweatshirt strode over, grabbing Belle's arms.

The hiker said, "Let go of my daughter."

But Belle kicked, lashing out with her legs, keeping her at bay, holding the knife at my throat.

My stomach lurched, and my mouth fell open. Could this older woman really be my mother?

Belle shoved me outside, pushing me toward an above-ground cement block cistern with a ladder going up the side. Rain poured down, getting in my eyes. My hair was sopping wet, and all I cared about was getting out of this alive.

I sobbed. Would this nightmare of a wedding ever end? I fought and kicked and thrashed, but she still dragged me up the ladder with the knife at my throat. Struggling with every ounce of my strength, I refused to be thrown in the cistern. I'd have to make sure she took my place. It was her death or mine on the line.

I gritted my teeth and pounded with my fists on her back. She yelled, but kept going, pushing me up the ladder. Sucking in a deep breath, I looked for a chance to turn the tables and maybe push her in the water. I screamed at the top of my lungs and dug my fingernails into her scalp.

53

KENDRA

I hurried outside following my daughter Claire, who was being dragged by a jealous ex-girlfriend. Why anyone would want Ralph was a wonder to me. He didn't lift a finger to defend his bride to be, and he looked scared of Belle. What a wimp, waiting for the police and not taking action. By then it'll be too late, with a crazed person on the loose.

I scanned the grass for a large slingshot I'd seen earlier and seeing it, I quickly picked it up, along with a few rocks. Lacey's plan to wreck the wedding involved using the sling shot she brought, but I'd talked her out of it when we spoke briefly by phone this afternoon.

Rain got in my eyes, and I wiped away tears. After all this time, I wasn't going to let some maniac hurt my daughter. Not on her wedding day, even if she was marrying a complete jerk.

I hurried over to the hulking evil-looking cistern, where Belle shoved Claire up the ladder. Claire's long flowing dress flapped in the wind. Claire fought with her fists and flailed, but to no avail.

"Stop right there," I called.

But Belle didn't look down or pause, pushing Claire toward her death.

I took a deep breath and put a rock in the pocket of the sling shot. Taking aim, I let the missile fly. But it sailed right past Belle and hit the cement block cistern, falling to the ground.

I yelled, "Get away from my daughter. Let her go."

But Belle continued shoving Claire up the ladder.

I bent over and found a heavier rock. Loading it, I aimed and fired on the mad woman. It smacked Belle on the head.

She turned toward me. "Stop that, or you'll be next to drown in putrid water in an old cistern."

Stalling her while I loaded my sling shot, I said, "What'd she do to you? Nothing. Let her go."

Belle snarled. "She messed with my life. Everything I thought was real was wrong. She deserves to die on what was supposed to be my wedding day." She took a breath and paused, panting hard.

I said, "You don't want that pathetic man back, do you?"

She pouted and shook her head. "No, I don't. But that

doesn't change what'll happen to her. Claire drove me to do this, and she's going under. Say your goodbyes."

Belle hurried up the ladder, shoving my daughter to the edge of the cistern. I loaded another rock, held my breath, pulled back the sling shot and released it, praying it would hit its mark.

The rock hit Belle's head as she reached the top. Belle slumped over with a groan and fell head first into the cistern.

Claire leaped away, clinging to the ladder, feet dangling in the air twenty feet from the ground. Claire hurried down the ladder and ran over to me, rushing into my arms, sobbing.

I patted her back.

A police officer in blue ran out, looking around. She said, "What's going on here?"

With a trembling hand, I pointed to the vessel of death. "A woman who threatened to kill my daughter fell in the cistern."

The officer pulled out her radio, called for backup and hurried to the cistern ladder, climbing rung by rung. Deep in my heart, I hoped Belle was dead.

54

RALPH

A guy with short sandy hair wearing a green apron came into the dining room, where I sat slumped in a chair. He studied the wreckage of the cake, soup bowls, and my tuxedo.

In a calm voice, he said, "Are you ready for the salad course? Or would you like another serving of soup first?"

I sighed and glanced at the empty chairs. My life was in tatters. I owed a ton on my credit card due to this disaster of a wedding. Nothing felt right about it from the start.

A female police officer came in the dining room, while the catering guy waited for my response. The officer said, "When the coroner arrives, would you direct him out back? I'll be outside securing the perimeter."

"What happened out there? Did somebody die?"

"Yes, somebody did, but I can't comment on the specifics."

Standing, I shook my head. Outside, Claire was talking to the older woman in hiking boots. I said, "Tell someone else. I'm out of here."

Filled with terror, I shrugged out of my stained, damp tuxedo jacket and slung it over my shoulder. Running out into the wind, rain lashed my face. I stood in the parking lot looking around. My wedding was ruined, someone died and I bet it was Belle, and my car was missing.

I smacked my forehead. I'd given the keys to Mack, and he must've taken off. I'd report it stolen and get the cops to track it down. I didn't care if it gave him a police record.

Candy, the events manager, came outside and rushed over, handing me an envelope. "Here's your final invoice. You'll find extra charges for broken dishes and additional clean up fees required. And if you ever decide to get married, please don't call us. Goodbye."

I ripped the bill up in shreds, letting the wind carry the pieces away. "I'm not paying for this. Give the bill to Claire. It was all her idea to get married here."

Candy said, "She told me just now to run it through your credit card, and I did. Have a lovely evening."

I stood dumbfounded in the rain, getting soaked. An unmarked van pulled up, and two men in hazmat suits got out, unloading a stretcher.

I said, "Do you know who died here today?"

A heavyset middle-aged man wearing black-framed glasses said, "Shouldn't you know, since you were here? Now get out of the way and let us do our jobs."

They trundled past, and I hurried back inside and found my suitcase, changing into dry clothes in the bridal suite. I pulled out my phone and booked a driver for a ride to Seattle via the Deception Pass Bridge. There was no way I wanted to stick around and see guests, if they ever got here. No one I cared about was waiting for a boat. All I cared about was getting out of here fast. I wanted to get home before Claire did to pack her things, setting them out in the hall for her to pick up.

The ride service texted and said a driver would arrive in an hour.

I clenched my fists.

Suddenly, the door to the suite slammed open, and Claire said to an older woman wearing hiking boots, "Wait here and don't let anyone come in until I'm finished with him."

55

CLAIRE

I marched into the bridal suite, slammed the door and blocked Ralph's way, putting out my arms with my back to the door. He said in a cold voice, "Get out of my way, Claire."

I clenched my jaw. "My mother's on the other side. If you make it past me, she won't let you escape."

He shrugged. "It's over. I'm going home."

"You're darned right it's over, but it's my home too. Don't touch my things."

He said, "I wouldn't do that. We'll divide everything up and take turns picking what we want."

I scowled. "I don't believe you. Give me your apartment keys. I'll sort stuff and tell you when you can pick it up."

He dangled his key in front of me, but when I reached for it, he snatched it out of my hands. "I won't fall for that and be locked out of my own place. How about you give me your key."

I crossed my arms and shook my head. "There's no way I'll let you get away with that. I'm keeping my key, and I'll come and go as I like."

He hissed. "I picked the place for us."

I glared. "You picked it, and I never liked it. I wanted to move, but you refused and said it was the best value in town. That was one more thing we didn't agree on. Tell you what, I'll let you out of this room, but you have to promise to move out tonight."

"Of course. I can do that."

My fingers twitched. I wanted to strangle him for inviting his former girlfriend to the wedding, not caring enough to rescue me, and for the weak, inept fool that he was.

He scratched a red welt on his wrist.

My gaze latched on the inflamed patch of his skin. "Did you go down to the beach at the cottage and get poison oak, you idiot? I told you not to do that before the wedding."

"Mack and I did, but it's a bit late to worry about that now."

I whispered a question I was compelled to ask. To satisfy my burning curiosity, I said in a low, urgent voice, "Why in the world did you invite that crazy person to our wedding? What were you thinking? Now she's dead, and it's your fault."

He shrugged, and I saw how cold-hearted he was under a carefully crafted caring exterior. He sighed. "She pressured me and insisted I invite her. I had no choice."

I swallowed and cut off a sob, seeing clearly who he was, swimming through life, taking the easy way out, looking out for himself.

I stood back and opened the door. "Today is the first day I caught a glimpse of how vile you really are. I guess I didn't know you at all. Goodbye."

He walked past me out the door, leaving as a stranger.

As he stalked away, tears trickled down my cheeks at the loss of a dream. My mother turned toward me, wrapping me in her arms. Patting my back, she said, "Oh, sweetheart, I'm sorry it worked out this way. But he's not worth it."

I sobbed. "I can't stand it when someone abandons me, like you did when I was little."

She pulled back, staring into my eyes. "Claire, I didn't leave you. Your father took you and hid you for years. I looked but couldn't find you. I tried to track you down. Believe me, I wanted desperately to see you and make amends."

I tilted my head, realizing what I'd been told might not have been the truth. My gut ached, and I clutched my churning stomach. Was it a dark fairy tale told by my father?

My mother said, "Will your father be on the first ferry over here, when it's finally fixed?"

"Yes, along with my bridesmaids, your mom and the guests."

She screwed up her face at the idea of seeing her mother. I didn't ask what that was about because my attention was diverted by two men wheeling a stretcher with a black body bag past us.

I sighed. "We're not getting married, and this is a crime scene. I don't want to stay here and relive this horrible day again with my friends. I'll call and tell everyone to stay on the Seattle side of the water."

Mom nodded. "Makes sense to me. Plus we have a lot to talk about, given the time we spent apart. I want to explain what happened to me and why your dad might've taken you."

I said, "Okay," but secretly doubted there'd ever be a palatable explanation for a mother abandoning her young child. There's just no excuse, and I wasn't ready to forgive her. It sounded like she was cooking up a story and blaming it on Dad.

56

FRANCESCA

I ran in the kitchen, my face wet with tears, and collapsed in my mother's open arms. I said, "I'm sorry, I ruined their wedding dinner. I spilled squash soup on the groom's tuxedo."

She patted my back. "I know. I saw. I went out when I heard the shrieks."

I stepped away, wiping my eyes. "Are you going to fire me?"

She sighed. "I'm sorry, sweetie, but I have to let you go. You're right, you're not the best fit for this line of work."

I sniffed and nodded. "I understand. I think I'll ask the garden store in Bayview if they're hiring."

She reached out and squeezed my arm. "That's an excellent idea. Let me know if you need a reference, and I'll say you were hard-working and cheerful with customers."

"Okay. Do you need me to stick around?"

"No, go home and recuperate. By the way, those two people ruined their wedding, all on their own, so don't blame yourself."

Taking off my apron, I handed it to her. "Thanks, Mom."

She patted my cheek, like she did when I was a child with a skinned knee. "I love you. You know that, don't you?"

I took a deep breath and blew it out. "Yeah. I love you too."

My brother came into the kitchen. "You off? Headed to create another disaster in your wake?"

I rolled my eyes. "Stop it. I didn't mean to spill the soup."

He grinned, running a hand through his hair. "Or the coffee, or the pop."

I elbowed Troy, and he stepped back, saying, "Be gentle with me. I'm younger than you."

Mom said, "Go on, you two. That's enough. Troy, ask the bride and her mother if they'd like salads and sandwiches, although I doubt it. A dead body puts a pall on one's appetite, I imagine."

I grabbed my purse and car keys, moving toward the door. "Bye."

Troy said, "Bye, Franny. See you around."

"Back at you."

I strode to my car, which was parked in a back lot, but

it seemed to take forever to get there. A man stepped out from behind a tree and said, "Hey, I need a ride to Seattle. Can you take me over the Deception Pass Bridge and down I-5?"

I stared at the groom, who was wearing a fresh set of clothes. "I can't do that. You'll have to find another way."

I jumped in my car, locked the doors and started the engine, driving away. As I passed him, he leapt out and pounded on my side window, screaming, "Take me to Seattle. I want off this island."

But I kept going, gripping the steering wheel tight until he was out of sight. Releasing a weary breath, I turned on music and let out a high-pitched laugh. What a weird day. But at least it was with family, which made it not my worst day, but an okay one. Maybe months and years later, we'd talk about this and bond over the strangeness that invaded our lives.

CLAIRE

I called my father. "Dad, I decided to call off the wedding and reception. Will you please tell everyone to go home? A woman just died, and I'm taking Mom to the cottage on Dirt Road for tonight."

"Someone died? How?"

"Ralph's ex tried to kill me. Mom hit her with a rock from a sling shot, and she fell in a cistern."

"Are you're okay? Do you need medical help? Is Ralph helping you through all this?"

I locked eyes with my mom. "He took off. He's long gone by now."

"What? I'll wring his neck."

Waving a hand in front of my face, I said, "It's just as well. I learned a lot about myself today and about him. It turns out we weren't meant to be together at all."

A police officer came up to me. "I need a statement from you."

"Dad, I've got to go. The police want to talk to me. Will you please tell Rhonda and tell her to cancel everything? Thanks. Love you."

Mom wiped tears from her eyes, and the officer said, "Is there somewhere we can talk?"

"Sure, let's go in here." I led the officer into the bridal suite, and we sat on a couch. My mother followed us and perched on the edge of a chair. It was odd to be around her after living so long without her.

The officer pulled out a notebook and pen. "Tell me how long you knew the victim."

"I didn't. I only met her this afternoon. I guess my fiancé invited her to our wedding, but he didn't tell me."

The officer screwed up her face and jotted down a note. "Isn't that highly unusual? He didn't tell you about this beforehand?"

I shook my head. "I didn't find out until she marched into the dining room and was yelling at him. She threw cake at him. I couldn't believe it when she shoved her hand in the cake, ruining it."

Mom said, "I think that's the least of your concerns today."

"Yeah, you're right. Everything I thought was a big deal before, like the rain and ferry cancellations didn't matter. But I learned a lot about Ralph today."

The officer said, "Take me step by step through the

incident. I understand the deceased dragged you up the cistern ladder and threatened you?"

"She said she wanted to kill me, and I couldn't get away from her. She was really strong, like she must work out all the time."

The officer frowned. "Do you think your fiancé had anything to do with her threatening your life?"

I tilted my head. "What're are you saying? That he might've had something to do with my death?"

The officer leaned in, a pen in her hand poised above paper. "Is that a possibility, do you think?"

Tapping my lips, my mind rummaged through recent events. I said, "He did insist on us taking out life insurance policies on each other, with a big payoff if one of us died after we were married."

"We'll look into it. Sometimes the people we least expect are capable of murder."

The officer scribbled something down.

I squirmed on the couch. "If he did, that would be cruel."

Mom and the officer watched me and didn't respond.

I whooshed out a breath. "He's totally self-centered, and I saw his true colors today. It's possible he asked his ex to show up after we were married. We were about to say our vows when two male strippers burst into the room."

The officer's eyebrows shot up. "Did you say strippers? At a wedding?"

I opened my hands. "I didn't order them. Lacey did. Mom, have you seen her around?"

She shook her head. "Not for a while."

I said, "Maybe everything went wacko when the wedding ceremony was interrupted, and it wasn't supposed to end this way. Belle was furious about Ralph leaving her."

The officer stood and pocketed her notepad. "We'll be in touch. Don't leave the area."

"We'll be staying on Dirt Road in a cottage tonight and maybe for a few days, if you need to reach me. But there's no cell or internet reception down there."

She nodded and put her hands on her hips. "It's an odd bunch living in the hollow. Are you sure you want to stay there? Locals tend to call us and complain about outsiders. We've had trouble before down on Dirt Road."

I smiled. "Mom and I will be fine, getting to know each other again, after a long time. I've stayed there before and can handle those people."

She handed me her business card. "My condolences for how your wedding went. Keep in touch and let me know if you go off island."

She walked out, and the caterer knocked. "Would you like dinner served?"

I sighed. "Now that it's a crime scene, I don't want to stick around, and I've cancelled the reception. But I'd like to take some food to go, if possible. My mom and I will be staying at a cottage off Sills Road."

A flicker of concern crossed the caterer's face. She said, "Of course. I'll bring it to you in a few minutes."

I held up an index finger. "Could we have bottled waters to take with us? The place we'll be staying has rusty-brown well water we can't drink."

She narrowed her eyes. "Are you by chance staying on Dirt Road in a rental cottage?"

"Yes."

"Stay safe down there. The locals get agitated by outsiders. I'll be right back with your food. Oh, and I thought you'd like to know I let the kitchen helper go who spilled coffee on your dress and soup on the groom's tux."

I shook my head. "I felt sorry for her. It worked out in a way and was for the best in the end. Don't worry about it."

58

BELLE

A rock hit my head, and I slumped over, falling. Gray, cold, grimy water greeted me as I fell into a cistern.

No, not this. I'm not the one who was supposed to die. It's her fault, and she's getting away with it.

But it was too late for protests.

My body hit the water and I blacked out, sinking down into murky depths.

59

RALPH

The events manager rushed out to her car, and I stopped her to ask, "What's going on?"

Candy glared at me, resting her hands on her hips. "What a mess you left. I'll have to hire a special cleaning crew. And the reputation of The Farm will suffer, given how your former girlfriend died on our property. Why didn't you step in and stop her from dragging your future wife up the ladder?"

I wiped a smile from my face, secretly pleased Belle died. Now she was off my back and not my problem. She'd been hounding me with emails I deleted before Claire looked over my shoulder and saw them, saying I had to break if off with Claire or she'd come ruin my wedding. But I didn't believe her or think she'd be as wild and ruthless as she turned out to be.

I cocked my head and squinted in the rain, telling a

bald-faced lie. "I was in a bathroom and didn't hear the commotion."

My best man Mack drove up in my car with Lacey smiling in the passenger seat. I said to Candy, "See you later."

"You'll be hearing from me if there are additional charges."

I trotted over to Mack, fuming at how he took off and left me with no transportation when everything fell apart. I'd lay into him and straighten him out once and for all.

60

MACK

I hopped out of Ralph's car, tossing him the keys. The events manager shook a fist at him and drove away.

With a wide grin, I said, "Lacey and I went out for a drive. Hope you didn't mind. It was crazy in there, and I couldn't take it."

Ralph crossed his arms, and his jaw tensed. "A friend wouldn't leave like that and take the car."

"It was just for a little while. No big deal, right?" I clapped him on the shoulder to take the tension down a notch. "Let's not let this get between us. It was just a stupid wedding, anyway."

He glared. "It wasn't just a stupid wedding, it was mine. You should've stuck with me until the end."

I shrugged. "Where's Claire? Did you get rid of the

crazy woman who threw cake at you? That cracked me up."

His eyebrows shot up. "She took care of herself, pretty much. She fell in a cistern out back and died."

I winced, rubbing my jaw. "Sorry we took off and missed it. Sounds like quite a scene."

Lacey said, "Where's Claire?"

Ralph pointed to The Farm. "She's inside. We broke up, and the wedding's off."

Lacey clapped a hand to her mouth. "Oh, no. She must be devastated. I should've stayed here for her."

I drew Lacey close. "Hey, we had to split. No one expected us to stay through that circus."

She slung her arm around my waist and nodded, with a look of guilt written all over her face.

Ralph threw his car keys in the air, catching them, and looking pretty happy for a former groom fresh from a break up. He said, "See you later. I'm out of here."

I hurried after him, tapping him on the back before he got in the car. "Hey, could I borrow some money? I'm fresh out until the next round of crowdfunding comes in."

His eyes narrowed, and he shook his head. "Sorry, buddy, but the wedding tapped everything I had and more. I'll be digging myself out for a long, long time."

My eyes flew to his pocket. "How about some cash? I'm broke, to be honest."

He tipped back his head and laughed. "Which comes

as no surprise. I mean, how many grooms have to buy their own best man's plane ticket?"

I held up an index finger. "I'm glad you brought up the subject. Can you buy me plane fare back to Thailand?"

He smiled. "I already did that once, and I'm no fool. Stop taking advantage of people and get a job."

Lacey strode over, taking my hand. "He's coming with me. He doesn't need a plane ticket to Thailand. He's going to do his podcast from my place."

Ralph studied us and nodded. "Glad to hear at least the wedding worked out for one couple. Don't call me if there's a wedding in your future. I'm done with weddings."

He hopped in his car and drove away. Lacey and I walked arm in arm into the building. I said, "Man, what a nightmare."

"You can say that again. I'm glad Claire didn't pick me to be her bride's maid after all."

I stopped in the hall. "Hey, where's your car? Let's just go,"

Lacey pulled back the hood of her cape. "I don't have one. I took the bus."

I ran a hand through my hair. She wasn't as loaded as I thought, but I liked her well enough to go along and see if it worked out.

Read a bonus epilogue (electronic format only).

To hear about new books, sign up for my author newsletter on my website at www.susanspechtoram.com

Next up is Book 2 A Chilling Christmas Eve
Francesca and her brother knew they'd be rich. But when their estranged father dies without a will, their wealthy grandmother leaves her estate to the gardener. Francesca flies to California to change her grandmother's mind and get the money she deserves. But the gardener has other plans…

Book 3 in the series: Poisoned Hollow!

Shore Lodge, a psychological thriller!
Her kids told her she was going to a retreat center.
But she ended up in a psych ward.
She must escape to rescue her dog and reclaim her home.

Follow me on BookBub for updates: https://www.bookbub.com/authors/susan-specht-oram

My Facebook author page is Susan Specht Oram Author

My YouTube channel features author chats, nature photography and audiobooks @susanspechtoramauthor

Thank you for reading my books!

ABOUT THE AUTHOR

Susan writes mysteries-thrillers and creative nonfiction. Previously, she served as senior director of corporate communications for biotechnology companies. Susan worked as an activity aide in an upscale nursing home's secure psychiatric unit. She was a potter and painter with an art studio in Seattle and has also worked as a market researcher, a nurse's aide, a waitress, and a library page. Her essays have been published in Mothering Magazine, Twins Magazine and Utne Reader. Susan grew up near Detroit, Michigan. She lives in a windy part of the Pacific Northwest with her husband and rescue dog.

Mysteries-Thrillers by Susan Specht Oram
- Shore Lodge
- The Thieves
- Cabin Eight
- The Mother's Threat
- Secrets at the Cafe
- Under Jackson Bridge
- Missing Man
- By Midnight

The Winter Storm
The Cold Night
Avalanche
These Lies
The Gas Station Motel
Wedding Nightmare
A Chilling Christmas Eve
Poisoned Hollow

Humorous fiction

Boating with Buddy, a report from a canine correspondent

Nonfiction

Personal memoir series: Strangers on a Train

Brief business books on investor relations, crisis communication and public relations

Strangers on a Train Memoir Series

Green Light
The Train
Canoe
Soup Kettle
Bathtub
Phone Call
Watering Can
Waterfall

www.ingramcontent.com/pod-product-compliance
Ingram Content Group UK Ltd.
Pitfield, Milton Keynes, MK11 3LW, UK
UKHW022237230426
12048UKWH00018BA/1309